LM KAREN

Summertime Lilies

A Contemporary Christian Romance (Oak Street Series Book One)

OAK STREET PUBLISHING HOUSE

First published by Oak Street Publishing House 2021

Copyright © 2021 by LM Karen

All rights reserved. No part of this publication may be reproduced, stored or transmitted in any form or by any means, electronic, mechanical, photocopying, recording, scanning, or otherwise without written permission from the publisher. It is illegal to copy this book, post it to a website, or distribute it by any other means without permission.

This novel is entirely a work of fiction. The names, characters and incidents portrayed in it are the work of the author's imagination. Any resemblance to actual persons, living or dead, events or localities is entirely coincidental.

LM Karen asserts the moral right to be identified as the author of this work.

First edition

ISBN: 9798389323223

Cover art by Dane at ebooklaunch.com
Editing by Michelle Schacht

This book was professionally typeset on Reedsy.
Find out more at reedsy.com

Dedication
To Brittany, whose perseverance and strength is inspiring.

Contents

Acknowledgement	iii
Chapter 1	1
Chapter 2	12
Chapter 3	27
Chapter 4	39
Chapter 5	45
Chapter 6	51
Chapter 7	58
Chapter 8	62
Chapter 9	74
Chapter 10	82
Chapter 11	91
Chapter 12	97
Chapter 13	102
Chapter 14	113
Chapter 15	117
Chapter 16	121
Chapter 17	131
Chapter 18	139
Chapter 19	147
Chapter 20	154
Chapter 21	161
Chapter 22	172
Chapter 23	177

Chapter 24	180
Chapter 25	183
Chapter 26	187
Chapter 27	193
Chapter 28	199
Chapter 29	206
Epilogue	210
About the Author	216
Sneak Peek!	218

Acknowledgement

This has been quite a journey. I cannot accurately describe the effort it took from not just me, but also from my favorite people to make this dream a reality.

Without Momma sharing her love of reading with me at an early age, I never would have discovered the joy I find in reading or writing. For giving me your eyes and sharing your name, thank you.

As I quickly realized at the start of the endeavor to publish, writing was the easiest and most enjoyable part of the process. The real work comes when the book is finished. Thank you to Daddy, whose steadfast support makes the world a little less intimidating. You delved into this world with me and without your sound advice and guidance, I would still be lost. I cannot thank you enough.

Thank you to Gina for being the first one to read my work, give me feedback, support, and encouragement. Thank you to Casey for being a close second, whose enthusiasm motivates me and keeps me going. You both are not only the best people I know, but you are also the best test audience I could ever ask for. Thank you for believing in me and being understanding through every declined invitation and canceled plan.

Thank you to Michelle for editing this book and making it readable. For helping me to be a better writer. Your time and effort are very appreciated.

Thank you also to Dane at ebooklaunch.com who created the cover design.

Chapter 1

Brittany

I am speed walking to the elevator after a twelve-hour night shift in University Hospital's oncology unit, trying to stay upright on my feet, when one of my direct reports catches me. This is both positive and negative—positive because the chatter helps keep me awake, negative because the chatter involves my employee complaining about her schedule.

Being a nurse is tough, but cancer patients are particularly challenging because they are long-term patients. We get to know them, we care for them through all the stages of their treatment, we celebrate with them when they go into remission, and we cry with their families if they lose their battle.

I happen to be a nurse manager at the Cancer Center, which is infinitely more difficult than just being a staff nurse. No one can prepare you for this role. I am basically the disciplinarian, therapist, mediator, encourager, and mother to a group of nurses who are both wonderful and enormously demanding. This has single-handedly been the most challenging experience of my life. I got my master's in nursing as a single mother and that was cake compared to being a nurse manager in the Cancer Center. CAKE.

Trish, the girl riding the elevator down with me now, is new to the team. We lost one of our veterans to an outpatient clinic in town, and Trish is fresh out of school. She is energetic and excited to be here, but is having difficulty adjusting to a full-time job.

Working at the Cancer Center is a little different because we not only have a unit in the hospital, but we also have an outpatient clinic where patients come to receive treatments. We usually try to keep everyone on their same shifts, but because we cover two separate locations, in a pinch, a team might have to rotate on swing shifts. It is just that sort of a pinch that ended up with my employees working swing shifts for about a month due to flawed scheduling on another manager's part.

I'm able to comfort Trish and get her to hang in there with us, assuring her night shift is temporary and occasional, not her new normal. I need to remember to put Trish on decaf beginning around 3:00 a.m. It is 7:00 a.m. now and she will never get to sleep judging by the caffeine shakes she's displaying. I've only been able to get out a few words of encouragement through her anxious chatter. She'll be useless next shift if she doesn't get some sleep.

I nod along with Trish as we walk through the lobby and toward the employee parking deck, giving her the impression I am listening, when I catch sight of someone familiar. Turning for a better look, sure enough, my second cousin stands in the lobby and appears to be getting directions. I turn quickly so she won't see me and proceed with Trish to the parking deck. Is that weird? I can't be the only one who resorts to duck and run in awkward situations.

Lily Young is my second cousin on my mother's side. We are the same age and grew up together until about middle school. Since then, we've avoided each other. I'm not entirely sure why. I think we just grew apart and then it got awkward. We didn't hang out anymore, but we were still around each other at school and occasional family functions. She got married about five years ago, around the time I had my son. I

CHAPTER 1

went to a bridal shower for her and I jokingly asked if she was ready for a baby. She laughed and said, "I'll do the married thing, you do the baby thing." I couldn't tell if she was slighting me because I had Grady without being married or if she was simply making a joke. Either way, I am sure we still have nothing in common and it's best to avoid her.

I make it home safely, though I was dangerously close to napping during more than one red light. When I work nights, my son, Grady, sleeps overnight with my parents. They conveniently live around the corner from us, so they can get him up and ready for school. I hate not seeing him in the mornings when I get home, but he has to be ready and on the bus before I even walk in the house. It's a huge blessing that my parents are so close and willing to help out.

Finally, after my twelve-hour shift, twenty-minute conversation with Trish, and a thirty-minute commute, I fall into my bed and let sleep take me. I don't even take the time to put pajamas on. It feels like too much effort at this point, especially when Grady isn't here.

* * *

Six incredibly short hours later I'm wakened by my blaring alarm, needing to get dressed and ready before Grady gets off the bus. Currently, that means I have an hour. After I hit the snooze button four times, I only have twenty minutes.

It's worth it. I roll over and hit the snooze again, despite the fact that it will leave me with ten minutes to shower and get outside to meet the bus. I quickly pull on shorts and a t-shirt, and by the time I run a comb through my wet hair, I can hear the bus pulling into the cul-de-sac where my house is located. I rush out the front door so my arms are waiting when Grady jumps off the bus.

He runs right to me and showers my face with sticky kisses, and, for a moment, everything in life is perfect. The school year is almost over, then Grady will graduate kindergarten and move into first grade. I am all too aware that I have precious little of these bus reunions left.

"Mama! I missed you last night," Grady tells me with his arms tight around my neck.

"I missed you too, Buddy," I say sincerely, soaking in the feel of his small body against mine.

The bus pulls away and Grady lets me go. "Look, Mama, I colored you a picture!" he says, proudly presenting me with a piece of construction paper.

I take the picture and examine it closely with a discerning eye, making a show of examining it. It's our house, a stick figure Grady on what I assume is his bike, and a stick figure me. My face blossoms into an impressed smile. "I love it, Grady, you did such a good job! I'm going to take this to work and put it up in my office."

With exuberant energy, Grady bolts into the house and I follow, my head turning when I see something move out of the corner of my eye. The movement stops with a pickup truck laden with furniture in the adjoining driveway. The house next door just sold, so this must be a new neighbor moving in. I file this away with an errant hope that there will be a playmate for Grady, not catching sight of the new owner.

"What do you want for snack, Grady?" I ask as I follow Grady into the kitchen.

"Cookies," he cheers enthusiastically with a hopeful smile.

I eye him knowingly with a smile playing on my lips. "How about I slice an apple and you can pretend they are cookies?"

"Okay." He shrugs off his defeat as I hand him a juice drink and begin to slice his apple.

"Mom?" Grady starts simply from his barstool as I work on the kitchen counter facing him.

"Yes?"

CHAPTER 1

"Do I have a daddy?" he asks innocently. My motions pause on the apple briefly in surprise before I collect my thoughts.

Grady's daddy is something we have discussed at length on a number of occasions. At the end of the conversation, he seems satisfied, but then a few weeks or months later he comes back and asks the same question. I haven't decided if this means he honestly doesn't understand or if he's hoping the answer might change.

"There is a man that helped Mama make you in her tummy, but no, you do not have a daddy," I say with gentle certainty as I put his snack in front of him.

"Alison says everyone has a daddy," Grady argues, seemingly confused.

I've been hearing about this Alison kid all year. Frankly, she sounds like a know-it-all.

"Well, if Mama ever gets married, you will have a daddy, but until then it's just you and me, kid." I move around the counter to ruffle his light brown hair, the same color as mine, and kiss his cheek. I continue to the kitchen table where he dumped his backpack to look at his folder from school. His daily assignments all have check marks, so that's good. Next year he'll start getting letter grades. Field day is Friday. I mentally check my schedule. I'm off Friday, so I should be able to make it.

The last day of school is coming up in a few weeks, so I will have to arrange some type of day camp for Grady while I'm working.

"Mama, can I go ride my bike?" Grady asks, having finished his apple slices with startling speed.

"Yes. Wear your helmet, and don't leave the circle," I remind him.

"I know," he assures me as he bolts toward the garage. I follow him and lift the garage door, making sure he gets his helmet on.

"Be careful around the new neighbor's house, Grady. Watch the truck, okay?" I warn again, eyeing the truck next door that has markedly less furniture in it now than it had before.

"I know," he calls over his shoulder in little kid annoyance as he pedals away.

I open the blinds in the front windows and clean the kitchen quickly while keeping an eye on Grady outside. I am so thankful our neighborhood is quiet and that we have this tiny, little corner to ourselves.

Well, mostly to ourselves. I peer out the window at the neighbors moving in next door. I hope it's a young couple. The two outside houses are retirees, who are great for keeping an eye out on the house and for Grady. I am in the middle, in the farthest corner from the outer road. The house in the middle next to mine has been a military family until recently when they were moved somewhere else and forced to sell.

I grab Grady's water bottle, one for myself, and an apple before heading to the garage. I have a decent size one-story, brick, ranch-style home with a two-car garage in the front. Getting a house with a two-car garage is the best decision I have ever made. My car fits nicely in one half with my grill and Grady's toys fitting nicely in the other half. I even have space to keep a chair setup so I can watch Grady while he plays.

I roll the grill out of the garage and fire it up, planning to cook some chicken for the next few dinners and lunches. As it heats, I head back into the house to prep the meat and simultaneously keep an eye on Grady. I head back out to the garage when I hear Grady's excited voice. He hasn't quite gotten the hang of volume control yet, so he errs on the side of shouting most of the time. I come out of the garage shielding my eyes from the sun. A guy I've never seen before is kneeling next to Grady and they're talking. New neighbor?

"Grady?" I call as I walk over to them.

"Mama, this is Matt. He's our new neighbor," Grady says with pride at having something important to share with me.

Matt stands as I approach. A baseball hat covers what I can tell is dark hair and green eyes shine out from under the brim of the hat. The

CHAPTER 1

combination makes me catch my breath.

I put my hand out. "Nice to meet you, Matt. I'm Brittany. This is my son, Grady, whom apparently you've already met."

"Nice to meet you, Brittany. Grady came over to introduce himself, although he told me he wasn't allowed to talk to strangers," he qualifies with a smile.

I let go of his hand and glance down at Grady who has already bored of the conversation and retrieved his bike to keep riding around the cul-de-sac.

"He's always had a little trouble with that concept. I hope he didn't bother you." Grady is so friendly that sometimes I worry he can be an annoyance to people.

"Not at all. Nice break time," Matt counters kindly.

He's handsome, and he's looking at me intensely. I forgo asking about his family in favor of getting out of there with my wits intact. "Well, it was nice to meet you. If you need anything, I'm just next door."

"Thanks, Brittany. Nice to meet you too." His friendly smile transforms his face and transfixes me for a half a second.

I shake myself and jog back over to my grill, finding it well heated. I run to the kitchen and grab the meat so I can get it going, almost plowing down Grady when I get back into the garage.

"Sorry, Grady, I need to get this stuff on the grill."

"Have you seen my water?"

I point to his water bottle sitting beside my lawn chair. "Remember that not talking to strangers means not approaching people you don't know."

He looks at me as if he's reminding me of something I forgot. "But you said I could talk to the neighbors."

He has me there. "That's true, you can talk to the neighbors, but if you don't know someone, even if they look like a neighbor, you shouldn't approach them. Okay? Not everyone is nice like Matt."

"Okay," he says with a frown as he works this out in his head. I have the distinct feeling we will have to have this conversation again. "I just wanted to know if there was anyone I could play with," he pouts.

The military family that moved had three kids Grady could play with, and he was devastated when he learned they were moving away.

"Matt doesn't have kids?" I ask casually, trying not to be interested.

"He isn't even married," Grady whines despondently. "He said it was just him, maybe a roommate. What's a roommate?" he asks while plopping desolately into my lawn chair.

"A roommate is another person that lives with you and helps you pay bills," I explain simply.

"Like a daddy?"

I frown. "No, a daddy would be a family."

Grady still looks confused, but frankly I don't know how to explain it any other way. "Hot dog or hamburger for dinner, Buddy?" Maybe changing the subject and avoiding this conversation altogether will distract him enough to make him drop it.

"Hot dog!" he shouts enthusiastically.

I chuckle, then tell him in a mild mommy voice, "Put away your bike and helmet, it's almost ready."

I tell him this now, even though I am just putting the food on, because it will take him at least another thirty minutes to get his bike from where he left it and wander back into the garage. Even if he's done playing and I tell him it's time to go in, he just has to play for another few minutes. Instead of rushing him all the time, sometimes I just let him do his thing and start prodding him a few minutes early.

***

After dinner, Grady helps me with the dishes before I get his bag packed for the evening. My mom will give him a bath when we get to her house, so I make sure I pack his Batman toiletry set. I take out his

CHAPTER 1

dirty stuff from yesterday and replace it with clean clothes.

"You almost ready, Buddy?" I call from his bedroom. Last I checked, he was in the living room coloring my dad a picture.

"Look at my picture, Mama." I inspect the drawing with interest. It's very similar to the one he gave me off the bus, except this one has a man stick figure in it.

"Who is this, Grady?" I ask pointing to the addition.

"That's Matt." He says this as if to say "duh Mom."

I bite back a laugh at his tone. "I love it, Grady! Great picture. Pop is going to love it."

I slip his backpack on his back and sling his small Spiderman duffle bag over my shoulder. "Come on, let's get to Gram and Pop's house."

Since my parents live just around the corner, we usually walk to their house. It's my final attempt to drain some of his energy before I drop him off for the night.

We exit through the garage, keeping the garage door up, and I don't bother to lock the door to the kitchen. Grady waves frantically to Matt as we leave the driveway and enter the cul-de-sac. It seems Grady has taken a liking to our new neighbor. Hand in hand, Grady and I progress up the road toward my parent's house. Matt drives down the street in a now empty truck, and Grady is beside himself when Matt beeps the horn for him as he waves.

As is our custom, Grady and I play "I spy" on our walk to my parents' house. It's been fun to watch him get better as we've played the game through the years. First, he picked the same things each walk. Now he is branching out and picking different colors and objects each time.

"Gram!" Grady calls and drops my hand to run full tilt at my mom. I'm sure her face mirrors mine when he does that with me.

"Grady! How was school today?" she asks with a big smile.

"Great! Look at what I drew!" He offers her his latest drawing proudly.

Mom inspects it and glances at me in curiosity when she notices an added man in the drawing.

"Grady, tell Gram who you met today," I prompt.

"Matt. He's our new neighbor. He's moving in today and he beeped the horn at me while we were walking here. He might have a roommate," he explains with excited authority.

Mom nods in understanding. "Well isn't that nice, Grady. Go find Pop and give him a big hug."

Mom hugs me while Grady trots away. "And how are you today?"

"Good. I grilled some chicken that I'm very excited to take in for lunch." I say this pleasantly because in my life exciting things are meal preps and new sheets. "How was your day?"

"Good. Not much going on for us this week," Mom says eyeing me curiously.

Unsure of the reason for her searching stare, I quickly move on. "I didn't forget the Batman toiletries tonight, so he should have everything he needs. Thanks again," I say giving her another hug.

Mom returns my hug, and we walk together into the house to catch up with Dad. I've always been close to my parents, but since having Grady, we have developed an even deeper relationship. They are quite literally my saving grace with their selfless care of Grady and myself.

After visiting with my parents and kissing Grady goodbye, I walk home and pack up for work. As I back out of the driveway, I spot Matt back with his truck laden down with more furniture. He waves, so I raise my hand to wave back. Then he pulls his sweat-soaked shirt off as he turns to head into his house. My car rolls slowly forward onto the street without assistance from the accelerator as I unwillingly gape at him, unable to bring my eyes away from his bare chest then retreating back. The new neighbor is hot. Really hot. Like, whoa.

Originally, I worried about Grady getting too attached, but now I'm a little concerned about myself.

CHAPTER 1

* * *

Matt

After hauling in the last load, I take a look around at the mess. Boxes and furniture are everywhere, but at least everything is in. I ignore the mess and put my bed together, adding the brand-new sheets my Mom shoved at me last week when she heard I was moving. Bed made, I trudge through the mess to the shower, hoping the hot water will ease my aching muscles.

I order a pizza and eat it on the front porch, surveying the quiet, new neighborhood. As proud as I am to own a house, I'm equally glad I got it on a cul-de-sac. I glance at the house next door. It also doesn't hurt that I have a cute neighbor.

Brittany.

Once again, my thoughts drift to her as they've had a tendency to do since I met her this afternoon. My heart stopped when I saw her waiting for the school bus with semi-wet hair, shorts, and a tank top. When that little, brown-haired boy with freckles launched himself at her, well, it was the most adorable thing I've ever seen.

I'm pleased I got the chance to meet the fun, little guy and his cautious mother this afternoon when the boy rode directly over to my house on his bike. I just happened to notice Brittany didn't have a ring on, but that doesn't mean she isn't with someone. I need to remember to keep my distance until I know for sure. Although, I can't help thinking about how interested Grady was in my comment about possibly taking a roommate. Best not to focus on this at the moment. I switch to mentally making plans for the rest of the summer, losing myself in decisions about updating the house.

Chapter 2

Brittany

A few weeks pass before I happen to remember I have a cute, new neighbor. Grady is out of school for the summer, and yes, I bawled like a baby when he graduated from kindergarten. Thank goodness I'm on day shift again for the foreseeable future, and Grady is now enrolled in day camp at the community center during the week.

We haven't seen hide nor hair of Matt, who seems to keep pretty much to himself. That's more than fine with me. With all of Grady's end-of-year activities, I've actually forgotten all about Matt. This is before around 10 a.m. one Saturday morning when I am making bubbles with a huge wand for Grady to ride his bike through. All of the sudden, Matt's door flies open and a perky blonde with a high-pitched giggle comes stumbling out.

"Goodness, Matty, since when did you get so serious?" she says in a sickly-sweet tone.

"Just get in the car, Kim." Matt doesn't sound pleased.

"Grady, come in off the road," I call to him somewhat worriedly. Six out of ten car accidents are caused by distracted drivers, and Matt seems pretty distracted right now.

"Oh, what a cute kid. I bet we could make cute kids, Matty," Kim says in a slurred purr.

I don't catch Matt's response, but I do get a glance of his scowl and notice the way he slams his car door. As entertaining as the morning show is, I hope Matt doesn't plan to parade a ton of hungover chicks through here, especially if they happen to drive themselves next time. I've never felt uneasy letting Grady ride in the street on our quiet circle, and I would hate for that to change. Grady rides his bike in the driveway until Matt's truck is angrily driven out of sight.

When Matt's truck is gone, Grady returns to the cul-de-sac on his bike, oblivious to any of the next door drama. I reluctantly get out the mower to cut my grass before it gets too hot. Really, I've waited too long already, but I hate cutting grass and I'm procrastinating. I always start with the back yard, because it's so much bigger, and I limit Grady to the driveway while I'm out of sight. I collapse into my lawn chair in the garage when I'm done, knowing I still have to regroup to cut the front.

"Mama, can I leave the driveway now?" Grady double checks with me, seeing I've returned from the backyard.

"Sure, Grady, but watch for cars," I say tiredly, now uneasily paranoid due to this morning's drama and noticing Matt's truck isn't back yet.

"I know," comes in his "I'm a big boy now" voice.

I don't bother rolling my eyes; he is saying this more and more. I eye the grill, thinking that burgers sound good for lunch but wondering if I have the energy to cook them. Downing the last of my water bottle, I get up and scan the street for Grady. Since recently mastering the bike without training wheels, I can hardly get him off it.

I gather my strength and start the mower, ready to get the front over with. *The sooner I start, the sooner I finish*, I tell myself. I'm on my last few passes when Matt's truck pulls down the street. I watch with proud approval when Grady pulls his bike to the side of the road, gets off, and waits for Matt to park in his driveway before hopping back on and pedaling away again. I can't stop a grin; I guess he really does know what to do.

I keep going, getting the yard done as quickly as possible. When I finally finish, I glance over and see Grady still riding his bike. I put the mower away and take a brief break, considering lunch plans. I could make us a sandwich or go with my burger craving and muster up the additional energy it requires. After pondering this for several minutes while I rest, I finally pull the grill out of the garage and fire it up. Since I'm covered in grass, I pull out the fold-up picnic table and put it in the driveway, hopefully preventing unnecessary mess in the kitchen.

"Grady," I call, and he rides over to me.

"I'm going into the house for a minute. Stay in the cul-de-sac and look out for cars, okay?"

"I know, Mom," he says, unconcerned with my repeated instructions.

"You did great when Matt got back. I'm proud of you for pulling over and getting off without me asking you to," I offer, hoping to encourage that behavior.

Grady isn't super interested in my praise, however. He is much more interested in trying to master the one-handed bike ride.

I jog into the house and mix hamburger meat together into patties. I head quickly back out to the garage when I stop short unexpectedly, almost dropping the plate. Grady is chattering away with a looming figure who stands just inside my garage.

"Hi, Brittany," Matt greets pleasantly.

"Hi, Matt," I say in surprise as I recover my balance.

"I was wondering if I could borrow your mower to cut my grass? I haven't gotten around to purchasing one yet, and my grass could use a cut," he asks nicely.

"Oh, um, sure. Let me set this down and I'll get it out for you," I say, gesturing to the plate in my hand.

"Mom hates cutting grass," Grady pipes in.

"Is that so? Well she does a good job, even if she doesn't enjoy it." Matt's kind words are colored with amusement at Grady's outburst.

I put the burgers down next to the grill and push the mower over to Matt, ignoring his praise. "It's nothing fancy, but it gets the job done," I say, almost apologetically. It's kind of a pitiful, gas-powered push mower. My dad gave it to me after he bought a riding mower, so it's easily ten years old.

"It's great for what I need. Thanks, I'll get it right back to you," Matt says sincerely, pushing the mower toward his house.

"No rush, we'll be here," I comment off-handedly.

I turn to put the burgers on the grill so I'm not tempted to watch him walk away. I'm still unsure about his suitability as a neighbor, so I probably shouldn't ogle him until I decide.

I jog into the house to grab the buns and toppings, then place them on the picnic table. When I clear the garage, I scan to find Grady, but my eyes land on a shirtless Matt cutting his grass. *Gracious.* I spin around and realize I have not found my child. I scan for Grady, careful to avoid Matt's direction. I finally find him, bike abandoned, crouched on the ground staring intensely. It's probably a lizard. I hope he doesn't end up catching one again. It took me weeks to find the one he accidentally let loose in the house after proudly presenting it to me in my kitchen. I shudder in disgust at the memory.

Thankfully, I hear the mower move to Matt's backyard, leaving me to relax at the picnic table without concern for my gaze. I check one last time on the burgers, flip them, and make one last run into the house for lemonade.

By the time I get back out to the garage, the mower is back in its place, and my neighbor's shirt is back on. *Thank goodness.* Although, if I'm completely honest, I have mixed feelings about this. Matt stands casually in my driveway, chatting with Grady. Trapped probably. The poor kid has taken to the man very quickly.

"How'd it do?" I ask as I set the lemonade on the picnic table.

"Great, thanks again. I appreciate it," He says with a grateful smile. He has a very nice smile.

"What are neighbors for?" I say lightly, my back on his distracting smile to remove the burgers from the grill.

"Matt can stay for lunch, right Mom? I asked him, but he said he wasn't sure you would be okay with it. But you are, right?" I look down at Grady's hopeful eyes. *Geez.* Thanks Grady.

"Um, sure. Join us Matt, if we aren't keeping you from anything," I say nonchalantly, placing the burgers on the table. This means my leftovers will be diminished, but if I am lucky, I will still get three to four lunches out of it. As a single mother, meal planning is fundamental to the health and happiness of all involved.

"If you are sure it's okay," Matt asks hesitantly.

Unsure of if he's hesitant because he doesn't want to or if he really isn't sure I'm ok with it, I simply answer, "Absolutely." Keeping my gaze on my task, I feel his intense eyes watching me closely.

"Grady, go get your bike. You know we don't leave it in the road. Then go wash your hands, please," I say to distract myself from Matt's nearness.

"Yes, ma'am," Grady answers quickly.

I cringe. He only says ma'am when I use my too-stern Mom voice. I soften my tone and say thank you. "I hope you like burgers," I offer Matt after Grady bolts for his bike.

"Who doesn't? This looks great. I hope you really don't mind. Grady asked and I didn't want to disappoint him," he confesses in a low voice to avoid Grady overhearing as he shoots past us and into the house, slamming the door.

I smile because I know the exact face Grady used on him. "I really don't mind. But please feel free to be honest with Grady if he is pestering you or talking to you when you need to leave. He is usually fine hearing

CHAPTER 2

no. I don't want him to bother you."

"Grady's a good kid," Matt confirms with an affectionate smile, albeit not responding to my comments.

I smile. Of course, I think he's the best, but I can go with good if that's all he's got. "Well, I think so. I'm afraid he is quite taken with you, so please, do feel comfortable telling him no if you need to." Since Matt was evasive the first time I said this, I feel the need to reiterate. Matt nods in understanding but again doesn't respond. I hope I didn't scare him, but Grady is quite taken, and he should be aware so he doesn't crush my son's feelings.

"All clean!" Grady announces as he skids to a stop next to me. He climbs onto the picnic bench and automatically folds his hands.

"Why don't you lead the prayer for us, Buddy?" I suggest, setting the meat in the center of the table and coming to sit beside him as Matt takes his seat across from us.

I fold my hands and watch Matt do the same with a fond smile on his face before I close my eyes. When we are ready, Grady begins singing "God our Father." I join in, and to my pleasure, so does Matt.

When we finish, I fix Grady's burger while Matt fixes one up for himself.

"Matt, do you have a daddy?" Grady asks suddenly, breaking the silence.

My hands hesitate and I stop myself just short of groaning, shooting Matt an apologetic look that I hope he understands. He glances at me briefly before answering, "I do have a dad. I would love for you to meet him someday."

I hope that will be enough to distract Grady.

"Do you have a roommate?" Grady continues his line of questioning. I sigh in relief and hope desperately we are off the daddy topic for now.

"Not yet. Not sure yet if I'm going to have a roommate or not," Matt explains casually.

"I'm glad it's not the girl I saw before," Grady says in great relief.

"Grady, that wasn't nice. Apologize to Matt," I admonish him, even though I agree with him wholeheartedly.

"Sorry," Grady grumbles in confused embarrassment.

"Eat your burger, Grady." I instruct as I make myself a burger of my own.

I throw an apologetic smile at Matt again, hoping he understands.

"That's okay, Grady. I don't like her much myself, if I'm honest," Matt says with a devilish grin just for my son.

I try not to delve too deep into Matt's confusing response. If he doesn't like her but took her home anyway, that doesn't seem good. It doesn't exactly seem like he had taken her home, though, as if it was his choice. I decide to focus on my burger instead of trying to work out the details. There's really only one way to know for sure, and I'm certainly not asking Matt about it.

"Mom, can I have another one?" I look over in surprise to see that Grady has completely finished his burger in record time.

"Absolutely. Matt, help yourself, as well." I fix Grady another burger and watch without bitterness as my future lunches disappear. Grady must be having another growth spurt.

"So, Grady, what are you doing this summer?" Matts asks in a friendly tone.

"I go to day camp at the community center while Mom works. They have a pool," Grady shares proudly.

"That sounds fun. Do you enjoy it?" Matt asks, further drawing Grady into conversation.

"Yeah, but Alison is going to camp at the Y, so I wish I was going there." Grady answers in disappointment.

I'm surprised at Grady; this is the first I'm hearing of this. "I thought your other friends were going to be at the community center this year?" I ask him.

CHAPTER 2

"Yeah, Tommy and Sawyer are, but Alison is going to the Y. Do you think I could go to the Y, Mom?" Grady asks, giving me "the look." His chocolate brown eyes are big and a little glassy, and he tilts his head in the way that just melts my heart.

"I'm sorry, Buddy, but I already signed you up and paid the community center. I thought that's where you wanted to be. You'll have fun with Tommy and Sawyer, even if Alison isn't there, right?" I say this hopefully. Part of me is glad he's not able to hang out with know-it-all Alison this summer.

"Yeah. I'll miss Alison, though." Grady says sadly.

Geez. I thought I'd have a while to go before girl stuff started. I'd hoped this Alison girl was just a fad and that he would forget about her over the summer. I'm starting to understand maybe that was too much to hope for.

"Grady, do you play any sports?" Matt asks, changing the subject.

Thankful for the assist, I don't begrudge Matt his third hamburger.

"I played T-ball this year. Mom says I'm a natural," Grady answers with great pride. I smile as Grady and Matt continue to chat about his T-ball experiences.

"Can we go swimming today, Mom?" Grady asks suddenly.

I hand him my phone after punching in the code to unlock my phone. "Call Gram and ask her."

"May I be excused?" comes his polite reply.

My chest swells with pride at my little man. I kiss his cheek and say, "Of course. Throw your plate away, please."

As Grady takes his plate to the trash can and calls my Mom, I lean in to speak softly with Matt. "I'm sorry about the daddy and roommate thing. He's on that kick lately." I'm relieved I have a chance to explain before he leaves.

"Not a problem. Hope I handled it okay," he asks uncertainly.

I simply nod before taking a bite of fruit, not really knowing what else to say. I mull over a way to change the subject, but Matt beats me to it.

"So, Alison, huh?" he asks with a playful grin.

I groan miserably. "I officially hate this girl. I have never actually met her, but she is constantly filling Grady's head with things he isn't ready for." I shake my head, warming to the topic. "I had no idea how he felt about her. He never once said he wanted to go to the Y, not that I would have let him follow the little troublemaker over there. I thought she was just some girl he saw at recess, but he seems completely infatuated with her. Almost as much as he is with you," I finish, sliding a glance at him.

Matt chuckles at my woes. "Ah, young love and a mama bear. This could get interesting."

Easy for him to say. I make myself feel better by officially taking some of his attractiveness points away just because I don't like how entertained he is with all this.

"Mama! Gram says we can, and Matt can come too," Grady calls excitedly.

I inwardly wince. Of course he spoke to Mom about Matt being over.

"Actually, Buddy, I'd love to, but can we make it another time? I have some unpacking to do," Matt speaks up gently as he rises to leave.

Grady looks disappointed, but then cheers up. "Tomorrow, okay? After church."

Matt laughs, enjoying his new little friend's enthusiasm I think. "Maybe, but no promises. I have an awful lot to unpack." Matt then turns to me and offers sincerely, "Thanks for lunch, Brittany, it was very good."

"Sure, anytime," I reply lightly with a little wave. "See you around."

With that, I allow myself the indulgence of watching him walk back to his house, maybe earning some of those attractive points back.

CHAPTER 2

* * *

The next week at work is a fairly easy week. Clinic duty is, on many levels, a much easier day because you are simply starting people's treatments and then letting them sit until the treatment is complete. Grady and I don't see Matt again all week, which is fine with me, but Grady looks for him each night. I try to explain that Matt is busy, but Grady insists Matt is his friend. I tell him that Matt isn't available to be his friend like his other friends that are his own age, but Grady won't hear it. I resolve to talk to Matt about this when I see him again to make sure he keeps his distance from Grady so my son's feelings won't be hurt.

Thursday morning in the clinic starts fairly easily, but that changes when I am notified I have a new patient arrival. All my other nurses are busy, so I grab the chart and proceed to the treatment area.

There are several treatment areas in the Cancer Center. Many are large rooms with big leather chairs spread out across them. There are TVs and small desks on rollers that can be pulled up to the chairs. Since the patients have to sit for long periods of time to receive their treatment, we try to make it as comfortable as possible. There are even some outdoor areas available during the cooler months.

I don't look at the chart until I got to the treatment room, but hurry to glance at it so I can call the patient by name when I greet them. I freeze when I see the name just as I enter: Lily Young. What is my cousin doing here?

I look up and see Lily staring at me red faced. She always embarrassed easily as a child; she was incredibly shy. As she got older, she remained shy, and her emotions always showed plainly on her face. I walk slowly over to her, my eyes never leaving hers. Thankfully, there are only a few other patients in this treatment room today, and they are well spread out.

"Hi, Brittany," she greets in soft embarrassment.

"Hi, Lily," I say stiffly with surprise.

"I heard you had gotten a job here. I think that's great," she offers sincerely. "I admire you for what you do. I know I could never be a nurse."

I sit down beside her. "Thank you," I murmur as I open her chart, not knowing what to expect but trying to process what this means.

"Brittany." I turn to her reddening face as she says my name softly. "No one knows about this except my husband. I would appreciate it if you don't share any of this with your parents or family."

I am stunned. She is closer to her parents than I am to mine. "Your parents don't know?"

She shakes her head. "You won't say anything, right? I don't want them to find out for as long as I can help it."

I stare at her in shock. *What in the world?* Then my training as a nurse kicks in and I am borderline offended. "Of course I won't say anything. I'm bound by HIPPA regulations. I take my job seriously," I answer brusquely.

She lowers her eyes in contrition, "Of course, I'm sorry, I didn't mean to imply you didn't."

Lily hasn't changed. She's just as soft spoken and embarrassed as ever. I look at her chart; skimming the page, certain words jumping out. Ovarian cancer metastasized into the intestines and lungs. Stage 4. Prognosis is twelve months. I glance at Lily in surprise. Her treatment is only a very mild hormone suppressant. This doesn't make sense. She should be on very aggressive treatments that target and kill the cancer cells. The treatment she's been prescribed will maybe slow the reproduction of cancer cells at best. At minimum, it will help keep her energy up as her body naturally fights the disease. I can't read her chart more in depth now; I need to get her treatment going.

"I'll be right back with your treatment," I say distractedly as I turn and speed walk back to the treatment depository.

When I arrive back, Lily has already peeled back the collar of her shirt, exposing her port. I start her treatment and escape quickly so I can read her chart more completely. It details significant growths in her intestines and ovaries. Most likely the spread of which was encouraged by the fertility treatments she's taken over the past year and a half, based on what I know of this type of thing.

So she was trying to get pregnant. Well, five years after marriage, I reason it is probably time.

I can't believe what I am reading. The severity of this illness is relatively rare, especially given Lily's age. It doesn't explain her treatment, however. I walk back over to her chair and sit down beside her. She has been reading a book, but puts it aside when I sit down.

"I'm sorry we lost touch, Brittany. How is Grady doing?" she asks with sincerity and interest.

"He's good. Just graduated from kindergarten. From Westmont, the school we went to." I answer casually as my thoughts and questions war with each other.

"Ah, Westmont. Those were good times. It's sad to think that Grady doesn't even know who I am," she responds wistfully.

I stay silent, assaulted by memories. Sleepovers, pool parties, playing wedding and teacher. "Why these treatments, Lily?" I ask softly, choosing the question at the forefront of my mind.

She heaves a deep sigh, as if readying for battle. "Think about it, Britt. The other treatments would have to be extremely aggressive, some even experimental. The cancer is so advanced there's a fraction of a minimal chance that aggressive measures would even help. And if they did, for how long? There is an equal chance, too, that the treatments themselves could kill me. Isn't the better option to spend the time I have left healthy and happy?" she finishes reasonably.

"But Lily, if you fight it at least you have a chance," I argue, watching her. She's so young, my age. I would be lying if I didn't admit a certain fear at the realization that it could have been me.

Lily smiles regrettably and shakes her head slowly. "It's not that much of a chance, Britt."

I sit back, my mind turning over her words. She's right. How many patients have I seen nearly die because of their treatment instead of the actual cancer? But then, how many of those people eventually came back in remission? Admittedly, it isn't that many, but it still happens.

Lily calmly waits for me to draw the same conclusions she's come to.

"Why haven't you told your family?" I ask giving up on this topic for now until I can consider it more thoroughly.

Lily face falls somewhat and she continues sadly, "They will be devastated. It would color everything between now and then, and I don't want that. They will worry and cry, and everything for the rest of my life would be about the cancer. I just want to enjoy my family. I want to make memories and have fun and give them as many wonderful things to remember as possible before I go. I want them to remember our last year together, all the amazing time spent together, and not remember the cancer. Maybe it's selfish, but I like to think of it as a gift I'm giving them."

It makes sense. I mean, hearing her thoughts on it I can completely understand, but how would her family feel knowing she was going through this alone? How would they feel knowing she chose to deny treatment and spend the year with them as normally as possible? Every bit of me is rebelling at the thought of not fighting by any means possible. Observing Lily, however, she is completely at peace. She has clearly thought this through. Not only is she happy with her decision, she also appears determined.

I know the patient has the right to make decisions about his or her own treatment. Still, it hurts to think of Lily not being able to live out the rest of her life, or even fighting for the opportunity. I remember the fertility treatments and realize her and her husband...I forget his name...will never have kids.

As if she can read my thoughts, she says with a sad smile, "I was kidding when I said I would do the marriage thing and you could do the kids thing, but now it looks like it's true."

I frown, not appreciating her attempt to lighten the tone of the conversation. Fighting for her life is not a joke.

"Sorry, too soon? I should let you process," she says quickly with a repentant wince.

I hear my name called from another nurse and get up to assist. I work with other patients for the next hour or so until Lily's treatment is complete. When I go to unhook the lines from her port, I can't help being assaulted by memories. I am suddenly sorry we lost touch too.

"If you need anything, Lily, feel free to give me a call. Let me give you my cell." I write the number down on a Cancer Center brochure and hand it to her.

"Thanks, Brittany. I'll be here every Thursday at this time. Stop by if you're able. I'd love to catch up." She offers this hopefully, then bends to give me a light hug. She is at least four inches taller than my 5'4" frame.

"Take care of yourself, Lily. I'll see you next week," I answer in agreement. Suddenly, after thinking of all the time that has passed, I want to commit to seeing her as much as possible before she is gone. That may seem odd when we haven't been close all these years, but I feel drawn to her.

I spend the rest of the day in a funk. It is hard to digest this news about Lily, and even harder to think I can't talk about it with anyone. I picked Grady up from day camp, pleased he doesn't mention Alison once. I pick up a pizza on the way home, not willing to cook dinner, and we eat it on the living room floor watching a movie. Grady falls asleep laying there. When I pick him up to put him in bed, I stand and stare at him for the longest time, thankful for the blessings God has given me.

Chapter 3

Brittany

Fridays are my favorite days. Who doesn't love a Friday? You've got the whole weekend ahead of you—no commitments, nowhere to be, complete freedom. I have worked through Lily's news enough for her to inspire me. She is choosing to live her last months on her own terms, and in her own way. Intentionally. Although it was hard for me to accept at first, I realized at some point as I was staring into the face of my angelic little boy last night that intentionality is something sorely lacking in my own life. I am healthy, I have a healthy little boy; we should make the most of our time together...especially since Grady still likes me. Soon there will come a day he can't stand me.

On today's drive to day camp I asked Grady, "If you could do anything in the world tomorrow, Buddy, what would it be?"

He is quiet as he considers his answer, and I try to guess what it would be. Putt-putt? Water park? Lake day? Trampoline park?

"I would go see Alison," he says with certainty.

Geez. I can't stop rolling my eyes in exasperation. Alison again.

"Aw, Buddy, I don't know how to get in touch with Alison's mom for you to see her." In all honesty, I am very relieved by this.

"Alison doesn't have a mom. She only has a daddy," Grady says matter of fact.

I don't remember anyone at PTO talking about a single father. I wonder if it's one of the "Alison has two daddies" type of thing. I bite back the snarky response of telling him everyone has a mom. After all, that's what Alison told Grady about daddies a few weeks ago just before school ended, which only spurred more questions from him.

"Sorry, Bud, I don't know how to contact her daddy. Is there anything else you would do?" I ask, hoping for something more within the realm of possibility.

"Get ice cream and go to the lake," he says this time.

That we can do. "Why don't we do that tomorrow, huh? Just the two of us?"

"Can we invite Gram and Pop? I haven't seen them all week," Grady complains.

I smile in acquiescence, "Sure, we can see if Gram and Pop want to come."

***

After work that afternoon, I practically jog out of the building at the end of my shift to pick Grady up, excited about our weekend of intentionality. To my unhappy surprise when I get there, Grady is not his normal happy-go-lucky self.

"Ms. Masters, Grady had a tough day," one of the camp directors informs me as I check in.

"What happened, Krista?" I ask, my mama bear instantly activating.

"He is smaller than the other boys, and they were hard on him today. Someone said something about his dad, and Grady got very upset. He ended up fighting with some of his friends. We separated the boys, made them apologize to Grady, and spent some time alone with him to make sure he was okay. Unfortunately, I think there may have been lasting affects for Grady. He took it pretty hard."

I listen to this, seemingly calm, but inside I am panicking. He is a little on the small side for his age. Not to mention this dad thing just keeps coming up. Will there ever be a time when this dad stuff will be okay?

I collect a sad and droopy Grady from his class. As soon as we're at the car, Grady climbs into his seat silently without looking at me. His face is drawn, and his motions are jerky with pent up tension.

"What do you want for dinner, Buddy?" I ask gently. Similar to his mother, you can tell a lot about his mood from the food he finds comfort in.

He doesn't respond.

"Chicken?"

No answer.

"Hot dog?"

Still nothing. Time to pull out the big guns.

"Mickey D's?" I offer hopefully and wait.

"Okay" he says in a small, pitiful voice.

"Do you want to play in the play place or take it home?" I offer. The play place at this time of day will be chaos, but if it would cheer him up, I'm willing to go with it.

"Home," he says immediately, with a sniff.

This is serious. He never turns down the play place. Ever. He didn't even consider it.

I go through the drive thru and add an ice cream, just for good measure. By the time we get home, he hasn't perked up at all and is completely unimpressed with the ice cream. I don't even have time to turn the car off before Grady jumps out, running head down out the garage toward the front yard.

"Grady?" I call, but he doesn't come, adding to his odd behavior today. I walk out front and call for him again without answer. I finally see him over in Matt's driveway talking with Matt.

"Grady! Come here!" I call more urgently, appalled at his behavior. I don't care how upset he is, it is unacceptable to run away and accost a neighbor. He makes no move to come back to our house, so I march with determination over to Matt's, frown in place.

"Grady Brayden Masters, come here right now!" I say sternly when I reach Matt's yard. I stop about ten feet away from Grady so he has to come to me. Grady suddenly has his fear face on, as if he just realized his actions. His eyes fill with tears as he slowly trudges over to me and mumbles, "Sorry, Mom."

"Get into the house this instant, Grady. Now. Go." I take the typical Mom stance, one hand on the hip, the other pointing toward the house. Shoulders slumped, tears tracking down his face, he walks slowly home. When he rounds the garage, my arm drops and my own shoulders drop.

"I'm so sorry, Matt. He had a rough day. I'll talk with him," I say without meeting Matt's eyes.

Matt sounds concerned when he says gently, "It's completely fine, Brittany. I was taking out the trash when he came over, no bother at all."

I pause for a minute; I'm not ready to deal with Grady just yet. After a moment, I heave a resigned sigh and walk toward the house. "Night, Matt," I say absently as I go.

"Night, Brittany," he returns softly.

I close the garage door and make my way inside. Grady is sitting on the couch sniffling. I take the seat beside him and pull him onto my lap. He comes willingly, wraps his arms around me, and cries on my chest. My heart breaks for him. When he calms, I say, "I know you had a rough day, but you can't run away from me ever, okay? You have to always come when I call. It's very scary for me when you don't."

I get a shuddered "okay" before I go on. "Do you want to talk about

CHAPTER 3

today?"

Grady trembles with tears and answers, "The other kids picked on me because I don't have a daddy. I thought maybe Matt could be my daddy. He needs a roommate, and you said you might get married someday."

I can't stop tears from flooding my own eyes. I want to give him a daddy. He deserves someone to play with, learn from, emulate. It's what every little boy needs. "Oh Grady, if I could give you a daddy, I would," I whisper brokenly.

"I know, Momma," He says with a sniffle.

"I love you to the moon and back, Grady," I whisper, my hold on him tightening.

"Can I just go to bed Momma?" he asks, looking up at me with watery eyes.

It's a tough day when a little boy chooses not to fight bedtime and instead asks to go to bed. I smile sadly. "Sure, Buddy. I'll come read you a story."

I read Grady three chapters of his Hardy Boys book before he goes out like a light. It is only 7 p.m., but with the first week of camp over and the hard day, I suppose he was due for a meltdown.

I grab the half liquid ice cream from the kitchen counter, take it out to the front porch, and sit on the swing. Grady's bedroom is in the back of the house, so if I truly want privacy or just need space, I come out to the swing.

Our front porch is fairly small, but it extends to the right of the front door. When I bought the house, I didn't think much of the swing hanging on the side, but it quickly became a solace for me.

The chains creak as I rock back and forth, shoveling tear-covered ice cream into my mouth. I cry for Grady, for myself, and for everything I can never give him. I can't bear the thought of my son suffering simply because he doesn't have a father. It's something so out of his control and hurtful already, it just doesn't seem fair for those kids to pile on.

The sun finally sets, crickets and cicadas coming out in force as the air slowly changes from thick and balmy to light and cool. I eventually stop sobbing, but the occasional tear still falls. The ice cream is long gone, and I am contemplating raiding the deep freezer for a fudge pop when I hear a noise. My head snaps up and I find Matt standing at the bottom of my porch steps. He watches me warily, like I am a bomb that could explode any moment. To be honest, though, the rabid hormones of a woman whose mama bear mode has been activated is pretty much the emotional equivalent of a bomb.

"Do you want a fudge pop?" I ask suddenly. I'm surprised to find him here. I'm very emotional, completely vulnerable, and he is incredibly handsome. A fudge pop seems like the most logical course of action at this point.

"I never turn down a fudge pop," he answers seriously. As if denying a fudge pop would be the same as denying oxygen to breathe.

With that, I sprint to the deep freezer in the garage and fish out two fudge pops.

"My emergency stash. Enjoy," I say as I hand one to Matt.

"I'm honored you would share your emergency stash with me."

"My son accosts you outside your home and asks you God knows what about being his daddy, I think you have earned a fudge pop," I say dryly. Maybe I should filter my words or soften my tone, but I can't find the energy to care. I can't help it. I'm spent.

"He told you about that, huh?" Matt prompts gently.

"Yep," I answer, allowing a pop on the "p".

We sit in silence, eating our fudge pops. I can't decide what it says about me that after the day I've had I'm distracted by his body being so close to mine. It's not a large swing, after all. My mind wanders as I calculate the last time I was in such close proximity to a man. Needless to say, it's been a while. I try to imagine what it would be like, to just be a woman on a date with a man, but admittedly I don't have a lot of

CHAPTER 3

reference information to go on.

"Do you mind if I ask what brought all this up today?" Matt asks softly.

His words bring my thoughts back to reality. I am more disappointed than I care to admit abandoning my daydream. I can tell where this conversation is going, and I need to decide here and now if I plan to bare my soul to this person. I guess he is an okay neighbor, but I'm not sure I want him to know my life story.

"Some bigger kids were picking on him for not having a dad. He is kind of small for his age," I explain shortly, still undecided about the rest.

The look of anger that flashes across Matt's features makes me respect him a little more than I did before. "That is a rough day," he says softly.

"He said he thought you could be his daddy because you need a roommate and I need a husband." I huff, "I mean logistically, he isn't wrong." I let loose a deep sigh. "Poor kid. If I could give him a dad I would. In a heartbeat." I wince as those last words leave my mouth unbidden.

Crap, I should have stopped with the logistics comment. I can feel it coming now.

"Do you mind me asking?" Matt leaves the question hanging.

Well, I opened the door. I can't very well complain he now wants to walk through it. I don't owe him anything, but after the nice guy Matt has been to Grady it may be nice for him to have the history. That or I'm riding a sugar high that will no doubt have me crashing harder than a car going ninety to nothing on a dead-end road.

"I don't know who he is," I explain with a heavy sigh. I could let him think the worst of me and leave it at that, but somehow that feels wrong. Eyes locked straight ahead, I try to stay as neutral as possible. "I was with some friends in college, just turned twenty-one. I only remember having one drink. Next thing I know, it's the following morning and I have no memory of the previous evening. Nine months later, Grady."

Matt is silent for several minutes. After six years of therapy, I can now successfully say I have moved on from that night and the emotions it dredges up.

"Wow, I'm sorry, Brittany," he says with compassion.

I shift awkwardly. "Don't be. Grady was unplanned, but I can't imagine life without him. He's turned out to be the best thing that ever happened to me. God has healed me from the past, and now I'm looking toward the future. I'm just sorry for what it means for Grady." Matt stays silent, not that I blame him. It's a lot to take in. I can't stop the bitter turn my thoughts take. "Stupid Alison. She told him a few weeks or so ago everyone has a daddy. Since then he keeps bringing it up."

Matt breaks the tension with an amused huff. "It all comes back to Alison."

Am I blaming my incredibly complicated life struggles on a child? Maybe. Not that I want to focus on that particular character flaw at the moment. A thought occurs to me. "So now that you know my life story, I think it's fair for me to hear a little about you."

"Do you now?" he asks with a challenging gaze.

"Don't you?" I question. "Before you start, though, I'm grabbing another fudge pop. Want one?"

"Like I said, I never say no to a fudge pop," he answers emphatically with a charming grin.

"Right." I jump up and run to the freezer, making a mental note to replenish my stash. I hand him one when I get back to the swing and relish the first bite. Ah, sweet salvation in the form of a perfectly fudgy popsicle. That's the thing about a good fudge pop. They aren't frozen, they're fudgy. That's a very important aspect to consider when searching for the right brand of fudge pop.

CHAPTER 3

"So, Matt I-Don't-Even-Know-Your-Last-Name, what's your story?" I prompt him lightly, ready for the spotlight to move on from me and my drama.

"It's not terribly exciting," he preemptively defends.

"I don't know, Kim seemed absolutely enthralled with you," I say slyly, baiting him. I can't help it. There are tear stains on my cheeks and I'm working on a sugar hangover that would rival Grady's the day after Halloween. I'm determined that he spills at least the equivalent amount of personal drama I spilled tonight, and the train wreck stumbling out of his house the other week seems like the perfect place to start.

He snorts. "I'm sorry you and Grady had to see that. Leftovers."

I wait, determined not to say anything else. Why am I suddenly nervous? I push away anxious thoughts with another bite of fudge pop.

"My last name is Knight. I am a teacher at Evans Middle. I recently bought a house, which I think you already know, and a lawn mower. I'm considering getting a dog soon," he adds lightly.

A teacher? Okay. A dog? That could go either way for me. Grady would probably immediately want one of his own and I simply don't have time for that. I nod along, wondering when we get to the leftovers part.

He hesitates uncomfortably before continuing. "Kim was my girlfriend in college. I partied a lot back then. About four years ago, when I started teaching, I straightened up, sobered up, and I like to think I grew up some too. I became involved at church, but I guess Kim didn't get the memo. She was home visiting her parents and thought we could pick up where we left off. Unfortunately, you caught me as I was taking her home."

I nod along in understanding. No one knows better than me that everyone has a past. We swing along in silence for another few moments. "Something is bothering me." I feel him tense beside me. "If you get a dog, Grady is going to immediately want one, and I'm not sure I can deal with a dog right now," I explain in consternation.

He smiles as the tension drains from his body and he counters, "Or it could help. Think about it. Instead of you getting Grady a dog, we can tell him it's just like having his own, only next door."

My pulse quickens at his reference to "we". "I'm not sure I could do that to you, Matt. You would never get him to leave," I say certainly.

"Every young boy needs a dog," Matt insists.

I snort, "Every young boy's Mom needs a housekeeper. I might have to go back on nights soon, and I definitely can't deal with a dog if I'm on nights."

Matt nods, "You're a nurse, right? That's what Grady told me."

"Yep, Cancer Center," I confirm.

"Do you always work different shifts?" he asks curiously.

"Not really. It just depends on patient load. We also have an outpatient clinic we staff," I answer easily.

We fall into a comfortable silence, nothing but the sound of the swing creaking and the cicadas singing. I think of mine and Grady's plans this weekend and wonder if it's appropriate to ask Matt about his. I wonder if the intentionality I have planned with Grady could be applied to Matt. With that, my mind drifts back to Lily, and an overwhelming sadness washes over me at the realization that I will have to watch her waste away due to her disease.

"I think I've lost you," Matt says quietly, turning to gaze down at me curiously.

"I'm just thinking about a patient," I answer without offering more. I'm not sure if I want to talk about Lily.

"It must be hard, working with cancer patients," Matt says with empathy.

He has no idea. "Some harder than others. It can be very rewarding when they go into remission or are cured and cancer free." I take a deep breath. "But yeah, it can be pretty challenging too." My mind drifts back to Lily, and I remember her as she was when we were kids. It seems I can't stop myself from talking about it. "One of our newer patients is a family member, although a relatively distant relation. She is my age; we grew up together."

Matt blows a breath out. "Wow, is the cancer bad or will she be okay?"

"It's pretty bad. She doesn't want her family to know about it. She's declined aggressive treatments so she can enjoy the time she has left." I pause. "I haven't decided how I feel about that."

In truth, I thought I had come to terms with it, but what if she could be cured? She is so young.

"I think that's pretty brave," he mentions thoughtfully.

I wasn't expecting this. I turn sharply and eye him. "Brave? Giving up is the opposite of brave."

He pauses to glance at me and then says, "I don't know that she is giving up. I mean, if it's as bad as you say, and the treatments would be that severe, maybe it's just acceptance. I don't think of it as giving up, not if she is embracing life in the meantime. To go through it alone so her family can have peace of mind for as long as possible? I don't know, but I think that's brave." He states this with a certain tenderness that gets my attention.

I hadn't considered that. I get it, I do, but...to not fight at all? "When my mind starts to go there, all I can think is that there's a chance though. However small, there is a chance that she could get better, and she is throwing it away," I contest regretfully.

Matt tilts his head in understanding. "It's going to be hard for you to watch her get worse."

He seems so caring and thoughtful. I look into his eyes for a second and see...what? His kind sincerity is uncomfortable to me because I'm not familiar with that from a man. I take a deep breath and wonder absent mindedly how long it will be before I discover his flaws.

"Well, I should get to bed. Grady wants to go to the lake tomorrow, and he will want to get an early start," I say as I stand, ending the conversation.

Matt stands too and nods. "Thanks for the fudge pops, and the talk. It was nice."

I nod, it was nice. Weirdly nice. Disturbingly nice. "Anytime." I stop and turn, "Oh, and Matt?"

He stops halfway down the porch steps and turns to look at me expectantly.

"Grady is getting pretty attached to you. I explained to him that you are very busy, but he insists you are going to be friends. I am trying to head it off, but you know..." I pause. How do I ask someone not to break my son's heart?

Matt clears his throat and looks up at me in the moonlight. Great, I'm going to be getting that image out of my head all night. "If it's all the same to you, Brittany, I'm the one who told him we would be friends. Grady's great, in fact, if I'm being honest, I wouldn't mind being friends with both of you," He states boldly.

I stand in stunned silence. He doesn't wait for a response, instead he continues toward his house, calling a "goodnight" over his shoulder.

I stare after him for several minutes before heading inside, locking up, and crawling into bed. I toss and turn, replaying our conversation all night. As if that wasn't enough, that stupid image of him backlit by the moonlight somehow filters into my dreams.

Chapter 4

Matt

I know immediately after tonight on the porch there is no going back.

I learned from Grady a couple weeks ago that they lived alone, so I have been keeping a casual eye out for an opportunity to see Grady and Brittany again. I had waited patiently, guessing that rushing them would be coming on too strong, but I never would have believed what happened today. I never would have guessed it would be Grady rushing over to pitifully ask me to take him and his mom on as roommates so he could have a daddy.

Brittany is a petite woman with an inner strength that is obvious. Every time I see her, she is a bundle of energy and purpose. It was sad to see her looking utterly defeated today.

My heart cracked wide open when Grady asked if I would marry his mom, so earnest and loving were the tears threatening his big, brown eyes. Brittany's eyes. Would it sound crazy if, for a moment, I wanted to tell him yes? 'Absolutely. I would love to marry your mom and become a family.'

Seeing Brittany wither then throw her shoulders back with determination and march into the house after Grady to do what needed to be done made me want to help. Be there for her. She's such a fighter.

When I heard the low groan of chains on her porch swing, I decided to check on her. Thank God I did, because there's no going back now.

As I'm getting ready for bed, my phone rings, distracting me of thoughts still fixed on my neighbors.

"Hey, Mads," I greet my sister on the line.

"All moved in?" she asks breathlessly. She must be running.

"Maddy, it's not safe for you to run this late at night," I say in my best big brother tone.

"I'm on my treadmill," she says with irritation. "Not that I couldn't run at the park if I wanted to," she finishes defiantly.

"Good. I am all moved in. Got almost everything unpacked and have all the carpet pulled up. So now I'm working on refurbishing kitchen cabinets."

"When can I see it?"

"When I'm finished with it."

"I could come and help, you know."

I groan. That would be a disaster waiting to end in stitches. "No thanks, Mads. I want to keep it a surprise."

She huffs, "You're just saying that because Mom will insist on seeing it once I've seen it."

"You're not wrong. When are you coming home next?" Maddy is a lawyer in Atlanta but visits regularly and is incredibly perceptive.

"That depends. If I come home next weekend, can I see your house?" she negotiates.

I smile admitting defeat. I could never really last against Maddy anyway. "Sure, Mads, just don't try to help me with anything."

She laughs heartily. "Deal. See you this weekend!"

I love my sister, and I'm excited for her to see the house. If I'm lucky, maybe I can keep her away from Brittany and Grady long enough not to scare the daylights out of the two of them.

My mind goes back to Brittany, and I immediately start making plans.

CHAPTER 4

This is going to have to be slow, serious. She has a kid, so I'll start small. I have a feeling that Brittany and Grady are worth all the thought and effort I'll have to give, so I gotta make this good.

* * *

Brittany

After an intentional weekend, I am feeling much better about life. Grady is back to his usual self, we had fun at the lake with my parents, and he is excited to go back to day camp. The only thing that didn't happen over the weekend was getting the grass cut. The weeds grow with startling speed during the blistering Georgia summer. I promise myself that I will cut the grass upon getting home after work today as I pull out of the drive.

I am relieved that I hadn't seen Matt around all weekend. I'm just not sure how I feel about our experience on the swing last Friday night. I don't usually spill my guts to attractive strangers on my front porch. I'm thankful for some time to think about it and get used to the fact that he now knows my life story.

I walk Grady into day camp with more apprehension than normal. I tell Krista we had a good weekend, but to please keep an eye on the vicious bullies who are tormenting my son. I do not vocalize the threat that if she doesn't, I will handle it myself, and she doesn't want that.

I get to work and through the day relatively easily. Hospital administration has decided to organize the oncology nursing staff into permanent placements in the hospital and the clinic. My team is chosen for the clinic. I am excited about it, but only because that means Thursdays now can be spent with Lily.

As I go about my work, I am too nervous about Grady's day at day camp to really focus on much of anything else. It is with great relief that I finally speed to day camp to find out how his day has gone. I am relieved that when I pick him up he is beaming. Good. He will be fine. No lasting effects of those other kids.

"Mama! We met a real, live fireman today! And guess what? I got to wear his helmet!" Grady's excitement positively overflows as he talks ninety miles a minute detailing every second of the experience.

Just like that I'm scanning his head for the possibility of lice. I will shave his head before I deal with lice again.

"Grady had a great day. Everyone seems to be getting along again," Krista assures me as she checks him out on the roster.

"Great, thanks, Krista," I say with a warm smile as I leave with my son.

I realize on the way home that I was so distracted this morning I didn't put anything in the crock pot for dinner. Sandwiches it is, although I remember I have half a watermelon in the fridge and my mood brightens considerably. Grady chatters the entire way home about firemen.

When we round the corner and the house comes within view, I am shocked to see someone has cut my grass. I assume it is Dad; he occasionally rides his mower to my house and cuts it for me. I shoot Daddy a text from the garage before getting out of the car and thank him. After following Grady into the house, I make the sandwiches for dinner and start planning out the rest of the week's meals. I hear my phone ding but wait until Grady's eating dinner to read it. It's Daddy's response: "I didn't cut your grass. Was I supposed to?"

Hmm. That's weird. I walk to the front of the house and peak out the window. Matt's grass is cut too, and now that I think about it, he did mention getting himself a mower. Did he cut my grass? I walk to the back of the house, shocked to find he cut the backyard too. That's impressive in and of itself because it's fairly large. I should tell him

CHAPTER 4

thank you, but I don't really like the thought of walking up to his house and knocking on the door. I have an idea that kills two birds with one stone.

"Wanna help me make cookies tonight, Bud?" I ask Grady.

"Chocolate chip?" he asks hopefully.

"Is that what you think Matt would like?"

"Yeah," he says with certainty around a mouthful of peanut butter and jelly.

I begin gathering ingredients and turn the oven on. I eat my sandwich while I work. It's always easier for Grady to help if I already have most of it done. When he finishes his sandwich, he comes around the bar and helps me dump things into the mixer. I work with him on numbers, getting him familiar with measurements as we go. When we finish, I have Grady draw Matt a picture and write thank you on it. Of course, it's adorable.

"Go up to the door and push the doorbell. Give him the plate and say thank you for cutting our grass, then come right back, okay? Don't stay." I look Grady in the eye as I instruct him while preparing the plate of cookies.

"Okay, Mom" he says in mild irritation.

"What are you going to tell him?" I ask. It's best to rehearse these things.

"Thank you. Then come right back," Grady recites dutifully.

"Thank you for cutting our grass," I say again. I have him repeat it a couple times before sending him over, praying he doesn't forget it all on the way.

I watch from a side window as Grady carefully walks the plate over to Matt's house, mindful not to drop it or spill. Is it chickening out to send your son over to say thank you to the handsome neighbor? Don't tell me, I don't want to know the answer. Either way, I hope the cookies make up for it. I feel a little guilty watching from the house like a creeper, but then I remember the cookies are still warm, and that I'm a single mom, and suddenly I'm ok with it.

Matt opens the door and gives Grady a huge smile. My heart tugs as Grady proudly presents the cookies and the card he made. Matt's eyes flicker to our house as his smile widens and he takes the plate of cookies. Grady is no doubt talking as quickly as possible in his excitement. Telling Matt he made the cookies himself, what kind they are, how he drew the picture, and which crayons he used. Matt is graciously nodding along as best as he can with a big smile. All I can hope is that Grady gets "thank you for cutting our grass" in there somewhere. My heart almost completely stops when Matt drops down to one knee and gives Grady a huge hug.

After that, Grady turns and runs back to the house, a bright smile on his face. I walk back to the kitchen as Grady comes in screaming, "Mama, Mama!"

"Did he like them?" I ask with anticipation.

Grady jumps into my arms and chatters excitedly, "Chocolate chip is his favorite! I told him I knew because we are friends."

"Good, I'm glad he liked them." I say, pleased.

"He told me to tell you thanks," Grady says as an afterthought.

I smile at that and start preparing our lunches for tomorrow, trying not to think about Matt anymore tonight.

Chapter 5

Brittany

"Tell me about your life. You know, what's been going on the past twenty years or so?" Lily demands.

I laugh as I hook the treatment up to Lily's port. "Not sure your treatment time will cover the past twenty years, Lil."

"Is there anyone special in your life...other than Grady?" she asks with great interest.

I inwardly groan. Really, the very first question?

"Nope, not really." It's true, but it feels like I'm lying. Weird.

Lily narrows her eyes and peers at me. "Really?"

I shrug and busy myself doing nothing of importance. I don't really want to go there with her right now, so I choose something else to start with. "I bought a house, I'm not sure if you knew that. It's right around the corner from Mom and Dad, so that's convenient."

"I heard that actually. That's impressive. I bet Grady loves it," Lily says warmly.

"He does. We are on a cul-de-sac and he just learned to ride a bike without training wheels. It's next to impossible to get him off it now," I say fondly.

I arrange the cords to be out of her way and put the IV on the rod connected to her chair. Instead of getting back to work, I sit down in the chair next to her.

"You don't have to get back to work?" she asks in surprise.

"I told my team I wanted as much time with you as possible. They'll come and get me if they need me," I answer casually.

"That's nice. I'm glad, Brittany, thank you," she says sincerely.

Are those tears in her eyes? Geez, I didn't mean to make her cry. "No big deal. You and your husband bought a house, right?" I ask in attempt to avoid further water works.

She bobs her head up and down. "Not far from you, actually. It's bigger than I wanted, but Joe loves it, and it is the perfect forever home."

Joe! That's his name! "How is Joe doing with all this?" I ask curiously. This is the first she's mentioned him.

Her face tenses and she bites her lip. "Not super well, actually."

"That's understandable. His wife is dying," I say compassionately. She winces at my words.

"True. He is still upset with me for not taking the more extreme treatments," she admits reluctantly.

"He'll come around," I say in an effort to be encouraging.

She looks hesitant. "I hope so. I had hoped he would've moved past it by now, but he hasn't. He is still pretty angry." She gnaws on her bottom lip nervously as I listen.

"It's just grief, Lily. He is losing you and you aren't doing anything to stop it. He is angry because he is grieving. Just give him time." I put my hand on her arm to comfort her.

She nods but her eyes fill with tears. "Thanks, Brittany."

I pass her a tissue and try to think of a way to change the subject. Before I can say anything, she wipes her eyes and says, "You know what would distract me from dying? Hearing about the special guy you lied about earlier." The corner of her mouth tilts in an unwilling grin.

I narrow my eyes. She couldn't even say it with a straight face.

"Seriously, Lil, that's bold."

She smiles unrepentantly. "You're the only one who knows about me other than my husband, and he isn't speaking to me at the moment. You are the only one I can manipulate. Come on, Britt, spill. I'm desperate for good news."

I roll my eyes. Geez. "I have this new neighbor," I start grudgingly, keeping my voice low.

"Oooh, a neighbor..." she says excitedly with a giggle, leaning toward me in her seat.

I hold my hands up and use my best mom voice. "I'm not doing this with you if you are going to act like we are kids again."

She claps her hand over her mouth in a show of seriousness. "I'll be quiet, I promise."

I eye her in warning before continuing. "Grady adores him. He moved in a few weeks ago. Grady invited him for lunch one day, and we ate at a picnic table in the front yard." I hold back the juiciest info, not sure how much I want to share.

She eyes me. "That's it?" she prompts.

"Well..." I eye her hesitantly. She no longer looks eager, more encouraging. It seems like she can sense it's difficult for me. I know if I told her that was all, she wouldn't push me. I take a deep breath; it may be nice to have someone to talk to. "Grady is obsessed with him. He had a rough day at day camp last week. Some of the other kids were picking on him for not having a daddy." I appreciate the way Lily's face clouds. "When we got home, he ran over to Matt, whose only mistake was to be taking his trash out. Grady asked Matt that since he needs a roommate and I need a husband, would he be his daddy."

Lily's eyes fill with tears again. "Bless his heart," she whispers sadly.

"Needless to say, I had a talk with Grady. It was a rough day and Grady wanted to go to bed early. So after he's in bed, I'm sat on my porch swing sobbing when Matt came up and sat with me. Thankfully,

I had stopped crying, but we ate fudge pops and talked, and it was nice. Then I got home Monday night this week and Matt had cut my grass for me."

Lily put her hand over her heart, telling me softly, "That is the sweetest thing I've ever heard. I can tell you like him."

I scrunch my nose in denial. "He is nice, but I mean, I don't even know him. And Grady is getting too attached already," I say nervously.

She tilts her head thoughtfully. "You have to be careful."

"He is really cute, though," I say with a grin, trying to lighten the mood.

A smile breaks out on her face. "I'll be praying for you, Brittany. You deserve to be happy," she says earnestly. "Have you dated much since having Grady?" she asks tentatively.

"Not really. I have gone out with a few guys from church...mostly just once each. I don't see any of them being a good dad for Grady, however."

Lily eyes me in concern. "Grady needs a good father, Brittany, but you need a good husband. If you marry a good dad for Grady but you aren't happy in your marriage, Grady won't be happy either." she points out.

"I know. It's just seems like a lot of pressure if I think about it too long," I admit with apprehension.

"Don't pressure yourself Brittany, you'll know." Lily reassures me with a warm pat on my arm.

Instead of arguing, I ask about her job, effectively changing the subject and giving us something to talk about for the rest of the hour. I'm glad I'm making this time for her. She's the same as I remember, but it's fun to discover the ways she's different too.

* * *

CHAPTER 5

When Grady and I get home that night, he spots something on our front porch. The second I park the car, he jumps out and races to the front door to find out what it is. I go ahead into the house to get dinner started, knowing Grady will bring in whatever it is. I'm setting the table as Grady slams the door closed and shouts my name.

"What is it?" I ask mildly curious.

"It's our plate," he answers. On the plate with the cookies that I gave Grady to give to Matt sits three citronella candles and a note.

"What does this say, Mama?" he asks handing me the note.

I don't make a habit of lying to my son, but just this once. "It says thank you for the cookies. It's from Matt."

"Why'd he put these on here?" Grady asks picking up a candle.

"He is just saying thank you. You should never return a plate empty." Not sure quite what to do with that information, he runs off to the living room for his two hours of screen time. I put the plate in the dishwasher, then walk back to my bedroom with the candles and the note. I sit on the bed and read the note again before putting it in the bottom drawer of my jewelry box. *For when we are swinging.*

My heart flutters and I peer out my bedroom window, which faces Matt's house. I sigh and am reminded of Lily's words: "You deserve to be happy." As I remember our conversation, I notice she didn't ask me if I liked him, she said she could tell I did. I smile to myself and wonder if Lily is exceptionally good at reading people, or if I'm more transparent than I thought.

So far, the time I've spent with Lily has been a blessing, each visit giving me something new to consider. I have an idea, corny though it may be. I'm sad we lost touch and I realize I missed out on what could have been a wonderful friendship. I dig around in my nightstand for a brand-new journal I purchased with the intention of starting a prayer journal...two years ago. I date the page and write my interpretations of mine and Lily's first visit, under lining the word "intentionality".

On the second page, I write her words to me today. The things I desperately need to remember: I deserve happiness, don't put too much pressure on myself, I need to choose a husband and not just a father for Grady. I take time to contemplate our conversations and wonder how Lily became so wise. If nothing else, this journal will be a memento to remember our time together before she passes.

After Grady's bath and bedtime routine, I stand in my room and contemplate the candles sitting on my dresser. Were they an invitation? Simply filling a need? He said "we" on the card, indicating an invitation, but I'm not sure how and if I want to respond. Instead of deciding tonight, I choose to leave the candles on my dresser to think about later.

Chapter 6

Brittany

I spend the next week staring at the candles and agonizing over them. I want to go and sit outside, in fact, I would have if the implications hadn't been there. I desperately needed space from Grady...just from life in general. I need my peaceful front porch swing. The thought of beginning a relationship with someone who will not only be with me for the rest of my life, but who will also be in Grady's, is just overwhelming. Grady already adores Matt. What if we start a relationship and it doesn't work out? Grady will be crushed, and I will have two broken hearts to deal with. Even worse, what if it doesn't end? Am I really willing to give someone else the right to parent my son?

It doesn't take me long to share Matt's gift and my agony with Lily when she comes in for Thursday's treatment. She immediately greets me by asking if I've seen Matt again, and the whole thing comes spilling out as I hook up to her port. To my utter shock and dismay, when I finish baring my soul like a basket case, talking fast and arms waving, Lily laughs—hysterically. I stare at her in disgruntled shock.

"Oh, Britt. Come and sit with me," she says while wiping happy tears from her eyes. I eye her, not sure I really want to anymore. Despite my new reservations, I sit while she calms herself and takes a drink of water.

"Can I tell you the quality in you that I have admired since we were kids?" she asks with a kind smile.

I watch her expectantly, curious to see where she is going with this.

"Your strength. I remember when I first heard the saying that dynamite comes in small packages. You were the first person I thought of. So small, but so strong. Scrappy, with so much energy. You would take on anyone and anything. Even when we were kids and our older brothers teamed up to torment us, you just looked at me and said, 'Come on, it's fine. They can't hurt us,' even though I was positively certain they could." She recalls fondly.

I'm stare at her wide-eyed now. I'm sure her opinion of me is skewed. I don't feel strong at all.

She takes my hand. "It's true, Britt. You were always feisty. It breaks my heart to think about what happened to you, but what did you do? You spent your pregnancy finishing college. You enrolled in grad school...*as a single mother*. You fought your circumstances and finished, graduated. Now look at you. You are a nurse manager in the Cancer Center, single-handedly supporting you and your son, fighting for his future. Then you go and you buy a house all by yourself," she says, clearly impressed.

After a pause, she takes a breath. "Brittany, you are the best mom to that precious little boy. Maybe he doesn't see your strength now, the way you fight for him and for your life together, but eventually he will. You don't even know how strong you are and how hard you are fighting, Brittany. That's what this is. You are fighting this thing with Matt because you can't say with certainty it's good for you and Grady, so you are fighting against it."

I keep staring at her from my chair. Is that what this is? Is that what I'm doing and why? "I have legitimate reasons though, Lil. I mean, I can't afford to just see what happens," I tell her, not liking the desperation in my voice.

CHAPTER 6

She waves a hand, brushing my words off. "It's not all or nothing, Britt. If you are hanging out on the front porch after Grady goes to bed, your son won't even know. If something happens and you break up, Matt's just your neighbor to him. You can wave politely and still let Grady talk to him. He doesn't sound like a guy who would turn Grady away after a breakup."

I weigh her words.

"Sitting on a porch swing does not mean you have to commit to a lifetime with him for you and Grady. I'm not saying not to be careful," she clarifies. "I'm just saying, stop fighting."

Sitting still, I silently digest her words.

"In other news," Lily starts, lightening the mood. I'm thankful for a change of topic. "Joe and I made up," she beams. "I thought about what you said. We talked. He is grieving. He isn't angry anymore though, so we can finally move on," she says with a triumphant smile.

"That's great, Lil. Glad I could help." I am pleased I've assisted her a little bit.

We spend the rest of our visit sharing about our week, our college experiences, and continuing to fill in the blanks. When her treatment is over and she leaves, I find myself looking forward to next week. I realize I'm going to miss Lily; it's going to hurt when she's gone. I try to remember our conversation as best as I can so I can write it down in my journal tonight. At least I'll have that.

* * *

As I pull into the driveway, Grady asks me about Matt. I answer lightly, "I haven't seen him, Buddy. I bet he is busy." Thankfully, Grady get distracted and doesn't ask any other questions.

I mentally make weekend plans as I get dinner ready and listen to

Grady play a video game in the living room. We eat dinner together, and I surprise him by giving him an extra hour of video game time after we eat so I can make another batch of cookies for Matt. He cut my grass again a couple of days ago. I won't have to cut grass this weekend and for this I am eternally grateful, despite the fact that his thank you cookies are several days late. What can I say? I'm busy.

I determine Saturday will be a desperately needed house cleaning day since I don't have to cut the grass. Maybe in the afternoon we will go to my parents' house to swim in their pool. I'm mapping out a potential schedule in my head as I plate the cookies. I save a few for lunch tomorrow for me and Grady, then get Grady in the bath and to bed.

I have already written down everything I can remember from my visit with Lily today, so without any other excuses, I grab the candles and the cookies and head outside to the porch. I light the candles, putting them on the white railing around the porch, then grab two fudge pops before sitting on the swing. I take a deep breath and allow the peace of the swing to loosen the tension in my shoulders. As we get deeper into summer, the air gets heavier and the days get longer. The sun is just now getting low in the sky as I rock back and forth, enjoying the quiet stillness of the evening.

I'm halfway through my fudge pop when I hear a door open and close next door. My heart starts pounding. He comes into view as he walks further out on his porch. Matt looks in my direction, although I can't see his features because he is backlit by the orange sunset. He walks over slowly, and I keep munching on my fudge pop to keep from passing out. He is more handsome than I remember.

"I had given up on you," he says hesitantly at the bottom of the steps. He waits, for an invitation probably.

It's not hard to gather my courage; I really do like him. "Not completely I hope."

CHAPTER 6

He climbs the steps and I can finally see his face; he's smiling. "Is that fudge pop for me?" he gestures to the treat sitting on the swing beside me.

"It is, along with this plate of cookies for you to take home." I take a breath and look into his eyes, then say, "Thank you for cutting my grass."

He smiles shyly before looking away. "It's no trouble. Gives me an excuse to use my new mower."

"I love the candles. It's nice to be out here and not get eaten alive," I say lightly to express gratitude for his unexpected gift.

He grins sheepishly. "I have to admit that was more self-serving than anything else."

"Oh yeah?" I ask, baiting him. Is that a blush I see creeping up his neck? I smother a giggle at his discomfort. This is fun.

"I was hoping, you know, we would be out here again. Bugs are fierce this time of year, though," he says gruffly, as if it were no big deal.

It is comforting to know I am not the only one who is nervous. His nervousness brings out the caretaker in me, and I want to ease his tension. "Grady asked me about you today," I say casually, offering a change of subject.

Matt gives me a small smile in what I think is appreciation for the subject change, which helps him relax. "Oh yeah? How is he doing?" he asks before taking a bite of his fudge pop.

"He's good. Day camp is going well. He made some new friends," I mention easily.

"How was the lake last weekend?"

I smile warmly at the memory. "Good. He loves the lake. My parents went with us and were there almost the entire day. My parents have a pool in their backyard, but Grady likes to play in the sand at the lake just as much as swimming."

"Do y'all have plans for this weekend?" he asks pleasantly.

"Not really. Since I don't have to cut the grass," I nudge his shoulder with mine in thanks, "I have decided Saturday will be house cleaning day. I have a ton of stuff that needs to be done. I might have my Dad come over to fix a couple things. We may go to my parents' and swim. Church Sunday. That's about it. What about you?"

"I've been doing some work on the inside of the house, updating it, that kind of thing. I think I'm going to take a break from that and do some landscaping Saturday. Spend the day in the yard," he says thoughtfully as if he's still considering the idea.

Dear Lord in heaven I hope it's hot Saturday and he does at least half of that yard work shirtless. "What kind of work are you doing to the house?" I ask to distract myself from that train of thought.

"Mostly cosmetic stuff. Cabinets, light fixtures, tile, bathrooms, kitchen appliances, floors, painting. That kind of thing," he says lightly.

"What are you thinking of doing to the yard?" I ask out of curiosity.

We continue to talk about the changes he's making to the inside and outside of his house for a little while. It is a safe topic that makes us both feel comfortable. I am slowly putting together tiny nuggets of truth about him. He likes doing the household projects himself, even if he doesn't know how. He likes a simple, warm design style, and he doesn't plan to live in the house forever. He's mentioned several times the potential resale value of the home after his upgrades. After talking about his house, we move on to other topics, still relatively safe but trying to get to know each other. We talk for at least another hour and a half until it is pitch black outside.

"Well, I hate to leave, but I know you have to work tomorrow. I should let you get to bed." He sounds reluctant, and I like that.

"You're right," I say, resigned. "Thanks for swinging with me. It was nice," I say shyly.

"Same time and place tomorrow?" he asks hopefully.

I hesitate for only a moment before confirming, "I'll be here."

CHAPTER 6

He nods his head once approvingly and starts to leave the porch.

"Matt, don't forget your cookies," I say as I walk to hand him the plate.

"Thanks, definitely don't want to forget these." He his hand brushes mine. There is something about his brief, feather-light touch that hits me down to my toes. I wonder if he feels it too, but the way his bright green eyes darken to emerald I know he did.

"Night, Brittany." His voice is low and intense.

"Night, Matt," I return softly.

* * *

Matt

Not gonna lie. The cookies are good. Really good. But really it's the sweet woman who gives them to me that makes me want to cut her yard every week. And she has a *big* yard.

I took a chance with the card. I have no idea how she explained it to Grady, but I thought I'd take the risk. After a full week of not seeing her on the porch at all, I thought I had completely blown my chances and chased her off. Then tonight I heard the low groan of the chains on her swing and found her sitting outside, candles glowing.

Just before I'd lost all hope entirely.

Yep, this is gonna have to be slow. I'll have to keep reminding myself of that 'cause I'm already looking forward to seeing her tomorrow.

Chapter 7

Brittany

When I get outside the next night, I find the candles are already lit, there is a fudge pop on the swing next to Matt, and he is smiling at me.

"Sorry, took me forever to get Grady down. Had to read two extra chapters of his book." I feel bad knowing Matt was out here waiting for me.

Matt's smile widens as he assures me, "No need to apologize. I got nowhere to be."

I sit next to him and tear into the fudge pop, glancing at him curiously.

"Can't have you providing all the treats," he explains with a grin.

I happily put the fudge pop in my mouth, savoring the taste.

"How was your day?" he asks me.

I groan.

"Tough, huh?" he correctly interprets.

I nod, never taking the fudge pop out of my mouth. I can't. I truly can't. I need it more than I need to vent right now.

He stays quiet until I can finally bear to take a bite and part with the rest. "Lost a patient. Two of my nurses called in sick. Grady pitched a fit about dinner; apparently hot dogs are now the worst thing in the world. Crappy day," I say before quickly pushing the fudge pop back

CHAPTER 7

into my mouth. My feet are still aching from the long day.

"That is a tough day. At least it's Friday, right?" he says optimistically.

I feel a mischievous twinkle in my eyes. "Thank the Lord! I'm not even setting an alarm tomorrow, and if I'm lucky, Grady will try to sneak extra screen time instead of waking me," I say with a sly grin.

Matt chuckles at my admission. "Still planning to do housework tomorrow?"

"Yeah, just sticking around the house, trying to finish cleaning up and getting organized before school starts back. Probably swimming at my parents' at some point. You?"

"My sister is coming to town. I haven't seen her in a while, so it'll be good to visit." He tells me with an excited smile.

"Where does she live?" I think it's adorable he's excited to see his sister. I can't remember the last time I saw my brother, much less was looking forward to his visit.

"Atlanta. She's a lawyer. She wants to see the house, so I guess I'll bring her by at some point."

"That'll be fun. She gonna help you decorate?" I ask conversationally.

He snorts in disgust. "God no. She's very...eclectic."

I laugh for the first time today. "Is that a nice way of saying tacky?"

He can't suppress his smile. "Maybe. Not willing to go that far, though. Well...maybe. She very into color. Lots and lots of color, on everything everywhere."

"That'll be fun," I giggle. "My brother is a cop. We don't see him much, but Grady adores him. Grady vacillates between wanting to be a cop and wanting to be a fireman when he grows up. He is inevitably all about cops and robbers after we see Derek."

We fall into a comfortable silence for several minutes, but I find myself wanting to know more about Matt and his family. "So, what are you going to do this weekend with your sister in town?"

He leans back in relaxation. "Probably the usual. Family dinner at my parents' house tomorrow night, I'll bring her by the house sometime after church Sunday, that kind of thing. I don't know when she's getting here, so I'll be around tomorrow morning until around lunch time."

I file that in my memory to be sure to peak out the blinds tomorrow morning. If he is doing yard work, sometimes he ditches his shirt, and I shamelessly peak out at him. My face heats as I desperately hope this is an option in the morning. It's supposed to be hot, after all. I remember the plea I sent to heaven last night that it be hot enough for Matt to lose his shirt working in his yard this weekend. Does that qualify as heresy? At the very least, I'm sure my Sunday school teacher would scold me for praying to ogle a man. I wonder briefly if that would be considered a sexual sin before Matt's voice breaks into my thoughts.

"What's got your face so red?" he asks teasingly.

I sputter and mumble something about the heat. He eyes me because he knows it isn't true, but my eyes are focused on my hands so I can avoid looking at him while I mentally use the force to try and melt away.

"Your parents live around here, right?" he asks, changing the subject. THANK GOD.

"Yeah, around the corner on Peach. They are on a beach trip right now, though, so we won't get to see them this week."

"It's great that they are so close," he says thoughtfully.

"Oh yeah, I love it. And so does Grady."

"By the way, how is your patient doing...your cousin, right?" he asks curiously.

I look up, surprised he remembers Lily. "She's doing well for now. She comes in every week for treatments meant to keep her body as stable as possible for as long as possible."

"That's good. Do you get to see her?"

"Yeah," I nod. "Actually, I usually sit with her during her treatments. It makes me sorry we lost touch. She's great. I'm really going to miss her."

He covers my hand with his and says, "It's nice you have this time with her, though. You'll have good memories to remember."

The heat from his hand goes straight through my entire body, and I blush again. "Yeah. I've been writing in a journal after our visits. Just things she says or things I want to remember about our time together."

He smiles, impressed. "That's a great idea. I'm sorry you have to think like that, though. That there is a time limit you have to consider."

"Yeah, me too."

My heart is racing. I feel guilty that he is being so sweet about Lily and all I can think about is his hand on mine. I watch with wide eyes as his gaze moves from my eyes to my lips, and my heart kicks up and races double time. He looks away and clears his throat, standing. His hand is still on mine, so I am pulled up with him.

"I should go. Let you get to bed. Same time tomorrow?" His voice is a little rougher than usual.

I nod, not trusting my words, then something clicks in my mind. "Wait, won't you be at your parents' tomorrow?"

He smiles down at me affectionately, and my breath catches. My, that's a sight. "I'll be here," he states simply.

He squeezes my hand and turns to walk away, leaving me to watch him as he heads back to his house. When I hear his door close, I finally release the breath I didn't realize I'd been holding. Wow.

I turn to blow the candles out and go inside when I notice that he brought back the plate from the cookies I gave him last night, this time with a box of fudge pops on it. I look for a note but don't find one, and am marginally disappointed. I take a picture with my phone so I can look at it later and grin goofily at the thought of Matt buying me fudge pops.

Chapter 8

Matt

Slow, slow, slow. I keep chanting this to myself after having come very close to kissing Brittany tonight. Did I see a little disappointment on her face when I didn't? I shake my head to clear it; I need to cool it before I totally run her off.

The next morning, I open all the blinds and get things cleaned up before Maddy arrives. I want to work in the yard today, but I want to see Brittany and Grady and I don't think they are up yet.

Yes. I'm waiting later in the day to work in the yard. In May. In Georgia.

I should definitely invest in sunscreen.

I am replacing the kitchen faucet when I hear Grady next door. I smile. The kid really only has one volume—excited. I peek out the window and see Brittany clutching a cup of coffee like her life depends on it, sitting in a chair in the garage, watching Grady ride his bike.

I finish with the kitchen faucet and open my garage door, smiling because I know by the time I get outside Grady will be waiting for me.

"Hey, Matt!" he says eagerly as I step out into the garage.

"Hey, Grady! How are you this morning?" I greet pleasantly.

"Good. Mom's a little cranky though," he says seriously.

CHAPTER 8

I smile in amusement. "Really, why is that?"

Grady cocks his head and gazes up at me in uncertainty. "I don't know. She was mumbling something about a fudge pop hangover, but we didn't have fudge pops last night. What's a hangover?"

I suppress a laugh and look down at him. I match his serious tone, continuing, "You know, I'm gonna let your Mom handle that one."

Grady moves on easily, unconcerned with my lack of answer. "Whatcha doin'?"

I survey the contents of the garage. That is a good question. "I'm gonna do some planting today."

"Plant what?" Grady asks, coming off his bike.

"See these plants here?" I gesture to the rows of potted azaleas that I'd picked up last week. "I'm gonna plant those around the front of the house."

"Can I help?" Grady offers hopefully, as if the only thing he's ever wanted to do in his life is help me plant azaleas.

"I'd love some help, but you should go ask your mom first." I like that he wants to hang out with me. He's a fun kid to have around.

"OKAY!" he shouts at the top of his lungs and runs back to his bike, pedaling away as fast as his little legs can take him.

I'm not at all surprised to see Brittany heading my way a few minutes later. She looks absolutely adorable with her hair piled on her head in a messy bun. I'm trying desperately not to stare at her toned legs because her shorts are Georgia hot-weather short. Her tank top is flattering too, and, all things considered, I'm proud of myself for plastering a smile on my face and focusing on her eyes. When I do, I notice she looks tired. There are dark circles belying her lack of sleep last night.

"Good morning," I greet cheerily. "Thought you were gonna sleep in?"

She glances bitterly at Grady and says, "Nope. Sure it'll be okay if he helps you? I don't want him to be in your way." There she goes, worrying again.

I smile as I assure her, "Nah, he's fine. It'll be great to have help, and we could use some man time, right Grady?"

"Yeah! Man time!" he cheers.

Brittany winces at his volume and I hold back a chuckle. She really is cranky this morning.

"Well okay, if you're sure...." She still looks uncertain.

I give her a wide smile and say, "Go get your stuff done. We're good here." With that, I turn and start hauling supplies out to the yard.

"Grady, I'll be in the house if you need me. Mind Matt and come home if he asks you to, okay?" she says in her mom voice.

"I know, Mom," he answers in a bored tone. "Go! It's man time!" he insists, practically pushing her back toward their house.

Brittany gives us one last uncertain look before heading back to her house and disappearing into the garage.

"Grady, wanna help me carry these plants out front?" I ask handing him an azalea.

"Yeah!" he reaches for it immediately, traipsing it to the front.

Once all the azaleas are spread out in the beds, I realize I may have been a bit overzealous in my purchasing. I probably have enough for the backyard too.

"Are we gonna do all this?" Grady asks with big eyes.

"Yup. You up for it?" I ask seriously.

Grady sets his chin in determination. "Yeah. I can do it."

I can't help but smile at his can-do attitude. It's good to see Brittany's strength in Grady.

"Let's get to it." I clap my hands and begin to explain the plan. "Now, where each plant is, we need to dig a hole, put the plant in, and cover it back with soil. Think you can help me with all that?"

Grady's chin slips. "It's a lot of plants..."

I nod in solemn agreement. "Big job for a big man."

CHAPTER 8

Grady sets his chin firmly again. "I can be a big man. Let's go!"

I grin seeing him step up to the task. "I'll start on the first hole, and you watch what I do, okay?"

It takes us one hour to do three plants. It's slow going because Grady asks a million questions. He insists on helping with the digging, saying he doesn't want to sissy out by just putting the plant in and covering it with soil. I have to hand it to the kid, when he sets his mind to something, he gets it done. I try not to focus on the fact that he is covered head to toe in dirt.

"Well, well, what do we have here?" I turn at the sound of my sister's voice.

"Maddy! What are you doing here?" I ask in surprise as I walk toward her with a big smile.

"I didn't want to take the chance you would change your mind about me seeing the house, so I drove straight here," she says with a smug smile. "What are you up to?" she questions, surveying the scene behind me.

"We are having man time!" Grady calls from behind me, working on another hole.

Maddy grins. "Man time, huh?" She looks at me questioningly.

"Grady lives next door. He's helping me do some planting this morning," I explain casually.

Maddy nods, but I can still see the question in her eyes. "You look like you are being a huge help, Grady," she tells him.

I turn to introduce them. "Grady, this is my sister, Madison."

Grady drops his shovel and stands, looking her up and down, no doubt distracted by brightly colored summer dress Maddy is wearing. "Hello, Madison, I'm Grady Brayden Masters. It's nice to meet you," he says formally, offering her his hand.

I smile because I know Brittany would be proud of Grady, except for maybe the dirt caking his hands. Maddy crouches down and shakes his outstretched hand, not even flinching at the dirt. "It is a pleasure to meet you Grady Brayden Masters. My friends call me Maddy."

He eyes her seriously. "Are we friends?"

"I want to be," she answers in the same tone as he observes her.

"Okay, but I'll have to check with my mom," Grady says seriously. Then, "You're very pretty." He is clearly taken with her perfectly styled hair and well done makeup.

Maddy laughs, saying, "Oh Grady, we are going to be great friends."

"Well, let me get cleaned up, and I'll take you in and show you around," I offer.

"But we aren't done yet," Grady says with purpose, "and my Pop says no man ever quits a job half done."

I glance at Maddy, not sure how to handle this.

Maddy grins, handling the situation effortlessly. "I'll just take a look around on my own, then come back out and hang out with you guys and watch you work. Sorry I'm crashing man time, though."

She doesn't really look all that sorry.

"It's fine. If I had a sister, I wouldn't keep her away," Grady says, unconcerned with the change in plans.

"Are you an only child, Grady?" Maddy asks with interest.

I glare at her in warning. Of course my sister would pump innocent children for information, but honestly, I'm not sure she can help it. It's the lawyer in her.

"Yeah."

"Your mommy and daddy must think they got it right the first time if they stopped with you," she says with a wink.

"I don't have a daddy," Grady said matter of fact, continuing to work on his hole.

Maddy doesn't say anything, but I can feel her gaze on me. I push the plant into the ground before looking up at her. She looks thoughtful.

"Hey, guys!" Brittany is coming toward us carrying a tray of

CHAPTER 8

lemonade.

"Brittany, this is my sister, Maddy. Maddy, this is Brittany, my next-door neighbor and Grady's mom." I am quick to make introductions as Brittany's eyes fall questioningly on Maddy.

Thankfully, her smile turns brilliant, "It's so nice to meet you."

"You too," my sister answers. "I was just getting to know Grady, although I'm crashing man time," she says in a stage whisper.

Brittany rolls her eyes in embarrassment. "Sorry, he gets excited to spend time with other guys. I brought you both some lemonade. I thought maybe you could use a break," she mentions nervously, offering the tray in her hands.

"Mom makes the best lemonade, Matt," Grady proudly announces, reaching for a glass.

"Both hands, Grady. It doesn't have a lid," she reminds him gently.

"Thanks," I say, reaching for a cool glass. A blush crawls up her face and I wonder if it's our close proximity, the way I'm gazing into her eyes, or the fact that she wishes I was working without my shirt. I grin and hope it's the last one.

"Let me grab another glass for you, Maddy," Brittany says before jogging back to her house.

I chug the first glass, and, indeed, it's the best lemonade I've ever had. When I finish, I find Grady working on another hole and Maddy watching me, her eyes dancing with amusement.

"What?" I ask.

"Just enjoying the show," she said with a wry grin.

"Show?" I don't like the sound of that at all.

"Trying to retain all the details to relay to Mom later," she says, grin widening.

I groan. "Maddy..." I say warningly, but stop as Brittany walks back up.

"Thank you, how nice!" Maddy gushes. "Come on, we'll sit on

the steps and watch the men work for a minute." Maddy takes Brittany's arm and leads her to my porch steps without waiting for her to comment.

I try to ignore them and get back to helping Grady. It seems like Maddy is intentionally talking low so that, with Grady and me talking, I can't hear much of what's being said. It doesn't help that Grady and I are moving farther away as we make progress down the house. I glance over every few minutes to see Brittany talking, listening, or laughing with my sister, and I can't help but feel both nervous at whatever Maddy is saying and excited that they like each other.

"Matt, you gonna put the plant in?" Grady asks, gesturing to the pot in my hand.

I shake myself, having been distracted again. I put the plant in and help Grady cover it in soil.

"Mom, can I have a hot dog for lunch?" Grady calls as he works with me on the next hole.

"Oh, sure. Gosh, look how late it is. I should start the grill," Brittany says as she gets up. "We have taken up all your visiting time, I'm so sorry," she says self-consciously to me and Maddy.

I snort. "Did me a favor really. Kept her out of my hair while me and Grady finished our man time," I say, giving her a wink.

Maddy laughs with genuine heart. "This has been so fun. You know, I just love grilled food in the summer. We never grill anymore, do we, Matt?" I groan because that's about as subtle as my sister gets. She's a lawyer for a reason.

"Well," Brittany hesitates, "If you don't have plans, join us. I have plenty. I would hate to interrupt even more of your visit, though," she says with concern.

Maddy jumps up with excitement. "We'd love to. Gosh, don't worry about that, I see him all the time." She waves at me while looping her arm through Brittany's and pulling her toward her house. My sister is

CHAPTER 8

a force of nature.

"Think we can get this done before lunch?" Grady asks. "I'm getting hungry."

"Yep. Here, I'll do the last three holes myself, and you plant and cover. It'll be faster."

Grady drops his shovel and does as instructed, loving the idea of being done with that particular task. When we are done, Grady props his hands on his hips and says, "We did good right, Matt?"

"No, Buddy, we did excellent! Thanks for your help. It would have taken me way longer by myself."

Grady beams with pride. "Can we do man time again?"

"Yeah, of course!" I laugh and ruffle his hair. "Come on, let's get cleaned up for lunch."

I take Grady into my kitchen and try to brush and shake all the dirt off him, enough so that at least when we sit down to lunch dirt won't fall out of his hair and into his food. I stand back and look at him when we are done. Well, I did my best.

I follow Grady over to his house just in time as Brittany is putting stuff on the grill. She has another round of lemonade waiting for us.

"Mom, can I ride my bike till lunch?" Grady asks, shoving a handful of grapes in his mouth.

Brittany nods yes without breaking the conversation with Maddy, and I watch in amazement as Grady takes off on his bike, once again trying to master the art of no hands.

"Feeling old?" Maddy bumps my shoulder.

Brittany laughs. "Ah yes, youthful energy. It's infuriating sometimes."

Tell me about it.

"By the way, thanks for letting him help this morning. That was really nice," Brittany says, glancing at me from behind the grill.

"Anytime. It was fun. Grady's a good kid and a hard worker. It was actually nice to have his help."

Brittany looks relieved. "Great!" I notice that she says this almost in surprise. Did she really think Grady was irritating to me?

"So what have you girls been chatting about?" I ask almost fearfully.

Maddy laughs evasively. "We've just been getting to know each other," comes her vague reply.

Honestly, I'm ok with it. Some things I'd rather not know.

"Did you know that Brittany leads a team of over ten nurses at the Cancer Center?" Maddy asks me.

"I did not," I say in surprise. I know she is a nurse at the Cancer Center, but I didn't know she is responsible for a whole team.

"It's true. And as nurse manager, she has to attend a gala at the end of the month, so she and I are going shopping tomorrow," Maddy says triumphantly.

Brittany looks a little guilty standing over the grill. "I tried to talk her out of it. I know I'm totally taking over your entire visit, but...well..." and she shrugs.

I smirk. "I get it. Maddy doesn't really understand 'no.'"

"Hey!" My sister pinches me. "Be nice!"

"Mama says we aren't allowed to pinch," Grady remarks seriously to Maddy, skidding by on his bike.

I turn wounded eyes to Maddy and watch her blush in embarrassment. "You are absolutely right, Grady, we shouldn't pinch."

Maddy offers me her apology. "I'm sorry, Matt." She kisses me on the cheek but pinches me under the table.

Brittany laughs with amusement as she put the food on the table. "Do I need to separate you two?"

Maddy just smiles brightly at her while I rub the second pinch spot.

"Oh, Brittany, I love these candles. Where did you get them?" she says, gesturing to the candles in the middle of the table.

"Matt gave them to us," Grady says brightly.

CHAPTER 8

Brittany flushes deep red, and Maddy turns twinkling eyes to me. "Good choice," she says, seemingly impressed. It irritates me that she thinks I don't know anything.

"Can we swim after lunch, Mom?" Grady asks.

Brittany gives a head nod. "Sure, Buddy. We'll walk to Gram and Pop's after lunch. That will free Maddy to finally visit with her family," she says with a guilty grin.

"Oh, your parents live near here, that's so sweet!" Maddy gushes.

"Yeah, it's great. They are out of town, but we have free use of their pool," Brittany explains gratefully.

"Next time I come to town, pool party!" Maddy suggests cheerfully.

"Maddy, you can't invite yourself to someone else's pool," I scold. Geez, she should know manners.

Brittany smiles, "We'd love to have you both. Maybe you could come to Grady's birthday party? We usually do a pool party at my parents' house for him and his friends."

"So fun! I wish I had a summer birthday. Mine's in February," Maddy responds, getting out her phone. "When is it? I'll check my calendar."

Britany gives her the date, and I check my calendar, too. Only a few weeks away. I put a reminder on the date of the event and go back to eating one of Brittany's burgers. "These burgers are delicious, Brittany."

"Thanks, I tried a new mix this time," she blushes in shy delight.

"I love it. I loved your others, too." I mention sincerely, hoping she might blush again. It's beautiful when she blushes.

"Mom, can I invite Alison to my birthday party?" Grady askes hopefully.

I watch Brittany tense. I think it's cute how much she hates this Alison kid.

"I don't know how to get in touch with her father, Grady. I would if I could." Grady looks disappointed, and I can tell it makes Brittany uncomfortable.

"I'm done, Mom. Can I go ride my bike?"

"Sure, Buddy. Stay where I can see you." Brittany sighs as Grady leaves for his bike.

"So, who's Alison?" Maddy asks in amusement.

"I really thought he would be over it by now. I guess I'm gonna have to figure out how to get in touch with her parents," Brittany says miserably.

Maddy giggles, "You hate this girl. Who is she?"

Brittany scowls in frustration. "A little know-it-all Grady met at school last year. He is completely smitten with her, and I couldn't be more irritated about it."

"Ah, young forbidden love," Maddy giggles again.

Brittany glares at her, which only brings more giggles from Maddy.

"So, Brittany, what church do you go to? I remember you mentioning before, but I can't remember," I ask, trying to save her from a merciless Maddy.

Brittany looks grateful for the change in subject, and we chat about our respective churches for a few minutes before Brittany rises to start cleaning up. We help her with the mess and get the grill and picnic table back in the garage so she and Grady can go swim.

"Brittany, it was a pleasure to meet you. I'll text you tomorrow when I'm on my way to pick you up," Maddy says, giving her a hug.

"Sounds good. It was great to meet you too. Have fun today!" Brittany returns her hug with a big smile.

I linger in the driveway while Maddy gets a head start to my house. "See you tonight?" I confirm quietly so I won't be overheard.

Brittany softly returns, "See you tonight."

I grin as I turn to follow Maddy.

"Whoa, what happened in here?" Maddy asks as I step into the kitchen.

CHAPTER 8

I survey the damage; yeah, it's bad. "I tried to clean Grady up some before I brought him over for lunch." There is dirt on every available surface, with plant limbs scattered on the floor. I have no idea how that even happened.

Maddy laughs at my incompetence. "I like them. It's good to see you show interest in someone."

"You sure made fast friends," I eye her.

Maddy's eyes soften. "I think she needs one." Then she grows smug again, calling like a little kid, "Can't wait to tell Mom!"

"Maddy." I groan. It is going to be a long day.

Chapter 9

Brittany

"Hey, Denise, I'm wondering if you could give me the phone number of Alison's dad? The little girl who was in Grady's class last year?"

I listen as Denise searches for the name and number in her phone, then jot it down, explaining Grady wants to invite her to his birthday party. When I get off the phone with Grady's former teacher, a wonderful woman who really encouraged him through his Kindergarten year, I stare at the number. Groaning in anticipation of doing something I don't want to do, I dial.

"Hello?" a brusque-sounding baritone answers.

"Hi, is this Alison's dad?" I ask tentatively.

After a pause I hear, "Yes...." He sounds, what, amused?

"This is Grady's mom, Brittany. Our kids were in class together last year," I offer, hoping that sounds familiar to him.

"Ah, Grady...yes, I've heard of him." The man sounds less than pleased.

I bristle. "Grady keeps talking about Alison too." I make my tone of disdain clear. However, I take a deep breath and carry on with my mission. "He would like to invite her to his birthday party in a couple weeks, so I called Denise for your number. We completely understand

CHAPTER 9

if you can't make it." I hurry to give him an out and pray he takes it.

"Brittany, right?" he asked, sounding amused again.

"Yeah," I respond reluctantly.

"I'm Gordon. What day did you say the party is?"

I give him the information and wait impatiently, praying he has plans.

"Well, we don't have a conflict." He sounds disappointed at that.

"Oh," I reply, sounding disappointed too. "That's great, I guess." I try to cover with optimism.

Gordon chuckles. "While I can't think of a reason not to, I want to really bad."

I release my own chuckle. "I want you to think of a reason really bad too."

Soon we are laughing together.

"I guess we will come, but only because Allison asks me about Grady every other day."

I grunt. "I get it. Grady keeps asking about Alison."

At least our misery is mutual. This actually makes me feel better about the whole situation. We hang up, and I consider my shopping trip with Maddy tomorrow. I am super excited, but chicken out on making sure she understands Grady has to come. A lot of my friendships didn't survive Grady's arrival, and I just learned to lean on him and my parents. I feel guilty enough to promise myself I'll text her tonight and make sure she knows.

After all is quiet after the day's rush, I type into my phone: Hey, Maddy! Excited about shopping tomorrow! Just want to make sure it's okay if I bring Grady? I don't have a sitter for him.

She responds immediately: Absolutely! The more the merrier!

I hope she means that. I look at the clock and usher Grady to bed, eager to get his nightly routine taken care of. Matt is waiting for me on the other side of the front door.

I step out and notice immediately the candles are lit and, once again, there is a fudge pop waiting for me. Matt of course, is waiting for me too, fudge pop in his hand and a smile on his face.

"Hey there," he greets warmly.

"Hey." I take a seat and unwrap my fudge pop.

"How was your day?" he asks in interest.

"Great! I got a few things done this morning, then I met this awesome girl who happens to be my neighbor's sister, and then Grady and I swam in the afternoon. It was a great day. Except..." I pause for dramatic effect.

"Except..." he prompts.

"I found Alison. Oddly enough, her father is just as upset about the situation as I am. Knowing he shares my distaste for the situation actually makes me feel better," I state smugly.

Matt chuckles at my admission. "The plot thickens. Is she coming to his birthday?" At my nod, he continues in amusement, "Oh man, I can't wait to see this."

I smile in good humor. "How was your day?" I ask, curious as to how the rest of his afternoon went with Maddy.

"Actually, not that great. I had a great morning hanging out with the kid next door, then my kid sister shows up and finds out more about my gorgeous neighbor than I know. Even gets her number. I'm actually pretty upset about it," he says teasingly despondent.

I laugh softly even as my heartbeat kicks up. "That is a rough day. So what are you planning to do about it?"

He grins mischievously. "Interesting question. I have a plan."

"Oh yeah?" I ask, in a challenging tone.

It's been a long, long, long time since I've flirted. I forgot how fun it is. "Yeah, gonna need your help though," he says with mock seriousness.

"I'd be happy to help. How can I assist you?" I offer, matching his tone.

"I need you to let me hang out with Grady tomorrow after church."

CHAPTER 9

Well, that's not what I am expecting to hear. "Oh, yeah?"

He sits back. "It's the crux of the plan."

"Well, if it's that important..." I start, suddenly unsure if we are still flirting or if he is serious. "Oh, I almost forgot, I'm shopping with Maddy tomorrow, so we won't be around," I say with disappointment.

Matt watches me carefully. "Actually, I was hoping you would let me hang out with Grady while you go shopping."

"Oh." I frown in surprise. I hadn't thought of that. I'm not sure anyone has offered to freely keep Grady for me before. "Umm...." My mind is spinning. "I don't know, I mean, I guess..." I can't force myself to go on.

"It's fine if you don't know me well enough yet. I'm just thinking about walking to the pond down the street and doing a little fishing. I thought he might like to come," Matt offers kindly.

Gosh, Grady would love that. So much more than shopping. I'm torn. Matt can tell I'm torn.

"It's fine, Brittany, we can do it another time," he reassures me.

"No one except my parents has ever kept Grady. Except I mean school and day camp," I rush to explain. Is it weird that this is a big deal for me?

He looks surprised, then thoughtful. "I understand, Brittany, it's fine, really."

He looks disappointed, which makes me reconsider. I let out a rush of air, gathering my courage. I know enough about Matt to know he is a responsible human being. He's a teacher after all. My heart might not be okay with him quite yet, but I'm sure my son would be fine with him for a couple of hours. "You know, Grady would really love to go fishing. So much more than shopping." I reason out loud.

"I don't want to pressure you, Brittany. The three of us can go another time."

"Just don't let him in the pond. It's gross," I say, wrinkling my nose in disgust.

Matt smiles brilliantly. "Deal." His eyes sparkle. "You know, I should probably have your number just in case."

I am beginning to appreciate his plan. "Of course, and don't judge me but I might need updates. Just depending on how long we are gone."

"Of course," he says with the demeanor of a soldier accepting orders.

I smile through my decision. It is fine. Really, it is fine. If I keep telling myself that, it will be. Right?

"You say that now, but he will try to con you into letting him into that pond," I predict.

"Duly warned," he says, then bumps his shoulder with mine continuing, "I can handle it. I promise."

We swing quietly for a few moments before Matt restarts the conversation. "So I knew you were a nurse, I didn't know you are a manager. That's impressive, Brittany. *And* you put yourself through grad school as a single mom? Wow."

I blush shyly at his praise. "It's what would allow me to make the best living for me and Grady. It's not that big of a deal. Lots of moms do that."

"It's a big deal," he says not allowing me to downplay my accomplishments.

Desperate for a change of topic, I ask, "How was the time with your family?"

Matt smiles. "Great. Fair warning, my mom might start buying things for Grady. Maddy spent the entire afternoon singing yours and Grady's praises, and my Mom is beside herself with joy."

I'm a little lost. "Why?"

He looks into my eyes, humor gone. "Because I like you, Brittany. And I like Grady. A lot," he says tenderly.

"Oh...." I blush in embarrassment and turn straight ahead, away from his intense eyes. The admission doesn't really sneak up on me or

CHAPTER 9

anything. I mean, I know I like him. I guess I kind of knew he likes me, but...to be outed to his parents...is this becoming a *thing*? Because I'm not sure I'm ready for a whole thing.

Matt's fingers find my chin and gently pull me to face him again. "I think you like me too, Brittany."

My heart is pounding and I can't feel my fingers. Is this normal? He smiles. I'm unsure why until I notice I'm nodding. Hmm. Do people nod involuntarily? I don't know if that's a thing.

"You can stop freaking out. We'll go slow." He sits back in the swing and puts his arm across the back.

I stare forward, taking a second to relax my ramrod straight back. While his arm is stretched across the back of the swing, he isn't touching me. I don't know why this feels so intimate, but it does. I can't even feel it back there, but I know it's there. I *know* it's there.

We swing for a few minutes silently as I will my heartbeat back to its normal pace.

"So," I say finally, "What did Maddy tell your parents about us?"

Matt sighs in what I recognize as long older brother suffering, "I should warn you, Maddy is very excited. She adores you and Grady, so I think she may have relayed every word said between the two of you, then I'm pretty sure she broke down the communication between the two of us by words, body language, and unspoken sexual tension."

I put my face in my hands in mortification. "Oh mercy. I can never meet your parents ever."

Matt laughs softly. "Don't worry, Dad and I talked about sports and upgrades to the house mostly. Mom is just as excited as Maddy and begged to go shopping with you tomorrow. Maddy saved you from that, though, insisting it would inhibit her bad influence on you. Oh, and my mom wants Grady's sizes so that if she sees something cute, she can buy it for him."

"Oh, my word. What is happening?" I ask in shock.

He pats my shoulder comfortingly. "They're a little...overwhelming. But they mean well. You'll never find more loving people."

I shake my head in wonder. "We aren't even dating yet."

Matt smiles. "I like that you said yet."

I clap my hand over my mouth. "I can't believe I said that out loud," I groan in embarrassment.

"Doesn't bother me. I have a plan," he stage whispers mischievously. Like the plan is top secret and a possible threat to humanity. Who knows? If it's a plan to date me, it very well could be a threat to humanity.

I huff, "You seem awfully sure of yourself."

His smile broadens, and it does devastating things to my insides. "The first phase of the plan is moving along better than expected."

"Oh, yeah?" I ask in disbelief.

"Definitely." He leans in like he is admitting a shocking secret. "I guess sisters are good for some things, but don't tell her I said that."

I laugh softly. "She won't hear it from me. So what exactly does the rest of this plan of yours entail?"

A sly grin fills his face and he curls his finger, indicating for me to lean in. He puts his mouth near my ear and whispers, "You'll just have to wait to find out."

I lean back in an exaggerated huff and eye my neighbor, although I'm pretty sure a smile is peeking through my set mouth. I face front again, but lean back into the swing, swaying gently in the moonlight with him by my side. I like that he isn't rushing me. I am enjoying the moment when fear crashes in and demands how long he'll be happy swinging on a porch swing waiting for me to get my act together.

I glance at him through the corner of my eye; he appears content. I swallow the fear and decide to stop fighting. I don't know what possesses me, but I verbalize my thoughts. "Lily told me the other day that I need to stop fighting. That I need to just let things happen."

CHAPTER 9

"Lily?" he asks, unfamiliar with that name.

"My cousin who is the cancer patient," I explain.

"Right." He is quiet for a moment. "So you told her about me?" he asks, sounding extraordinarily pleased.

I don't look at him, but I know he is smiling. "I did. I told her about the candles, and about how I stared at them for a week without coming out here even though I desperately wanted to but I wasn't sure if I was ready for what waited for me." I can't keep the vulnerability from my eyes, face, and voice.

His eyes soften, and he opens his mouth to say something, then stops. I pick up the thought instead. "I just want you to know, I'm going to try...to stop fighting. It just may be...a process."

Warmly he says, "It's, okay Brittany. We'll go at your pace. I'm not rushing anything."

I appreciate the sincerity.

"Why do you look surprised?" he asks suddenly.

I look at my hands in uncertainty. "I have about thirty reasons to be flat-out shocked right now." The irony strikes me immediately. "The main reason is I've never met anyone like you. Ever. I'm only wondering when you are going to wake up and realize the single mom and boy next door aren't worth all this trouble," I say in self-deprecation.

To my surprise, Matt pats my shoulder for the second time tonight with true affection. "Oh Brittany, you have a lot to learn. Don't you worry, I have a plan."

Chapter 10

Brittany

I gasp for breath as tears rolled down my cheeks. "Stop! I can't take any more!" I gulp through gales of laughter.

Maddy snorts, "I wish I could stop. That doesn't even cover last month. Unfortunately, my sordid dating history goes on much longer."

I try to calm myself. We found the perfect dress about an hour and a half into our shopping excursion, so as a reward we now sit in a muted but cozy coffee shop.

"What about you?" Maddy inquires curiously.

I am still wiping tears away as I admit, "I don't date. Unfortunately, this is a conversation you'll have to carry yourself."

Maddy eyes me doubtfully. "Come on, not ever?"

"If I tell you, will it get back to Matt and your parents?" I ask calling her out.

Maddy winces. "Man, sold out by my own brother."

I smile playfully. "That's what I thought."

Maddy's eyes light up with an idea. "Tell you what, for everything you tell me, I'll tell you about Matt."

I consider this. He already has insider information on me, it wouldn't hurt to level the playing field. I hold out my hand. "Deal. But I'm afraid

CHAPTER 10

I end up on the better side of the arrangement because I really have only had about three dates in six years."

Maddy's eyes bug. "Three dates in six years?! What in the world? You are hot!" she says with uncomfortably loud enthusiasm.

I laugh awkwardly, countering, "Maybe, but I'm a single mom, and it's actually entertaining to see the trail blazed by a man running away from me when he hears those words."

Maddy rolls her eyes, agreeing. "Men are stupid. So what happened on the three dates?"

I wave a hand dismissively. "One and done. Guys from my church. I probably wouldn't have even gone out, but I felt pressured by my parents or someone from the church. Nothing entertaining, just...not right."

"And then you met the boy next door," she fills in dreamily.

"Something like that," I giggle. "Actually, I think my son met our new neighbor, asked him to be my husband, and said neighbor took pity on a sobbing woman on her front porch one evening."

Maddy's face lights up, listening ears clearly on. "Now *that* story sounds fascinating."

I narrow my eyes at her. "You know, I just realized you never did confirm nor deny what would make it back to your parents."

Maddy looks a little guilty. "I'll gloss over the good stuff. It's mostly because we are so excited Matt is finally showing interest in someone." She awkwardly admits, "We have a tendency to get a little carried away."

"Matt doesn't date much either?" I ask, skillfully steering the subject to him.

Maddy leans in closer and speaks in a low voice as if she's spilling all Matt's secrets. "He was engaged a few years ago. Didn't end well. She ran off with his best friend. Matt was never really the same after that."

I am quiet, digesting this. Then Maddy looks thoughtful. "I think it hurt him more deeply than we realized. You know, Matt can be the strong, silent type, but when he opens up to someone, it's like that person permanently changes him. He feels very deeply."

I nod slowly, taking this in.

"Even if I didn't completely adore my brother and think the world of him, that's how I know he will do right by you and Grady," Maddy says with conviction.

I smile at her confidence. I wish I shared that confidence, but then, and for the first time, I'm on my way to doing just that. My phone dings and I dig it out of my purse; Matt has been religiously sending me photo updates every thirty minutes. I gasp as I open the new message. Instead of a photo of just Grady, it's a photo of Matt and Grady smiling widely at the camera with the pond in the background.

I show it to Maddy. "Aw! I love that! Matt's always been great with kids. I think that's why he went into teaching."

I gaze at the photo and sent a brief reply before putting my phone away. "You know, I can't remember when I've laughed as hard as I did today."

Maddy smiles proudly. "That's me, your friendly, everyday, source of entertainment."

"How much does Matt know about your sordid dating history?" I ask coyly.

Maddy pales. "You wouldn't do that to me, right Britt? I mean, I thought we were becoming friends and everything," she says feigning shock. "Matt takes protective older brother to a new level."

I grin, finally having something on her. "Tell you what, our conversations today stay between us. *Just* us," I say pointedly.

Maddy looks guilty again. "I said I'd gloss over," she says defensively.

I guess that's just the best I'm gonna get from her, so I go with it. "Come on, let's go home. Thanks for helping me find a dress. I probably never would have tried that one on, but it's perfect."

We chat as we drive back to the house, and I smile when I see Grady

CHAPTER 10

riding his bike and Matt sitting outside watching him.

"Mom! Mom, Mom, Mom! Guess what?" Grady is shouting animatedly before my car door even opens.

"What?" I ask with an amused smile.

"Matt took me fishing! I went fishing Mom!" Grady says like he personally landed a spaceship on the moon, with all the pride and enthusiasm that entails.

My boy is so excited I can't help but laugh. "I know! I saw the pictures. Did you have fun?"

It seems like a rhetorical question at this point, but he clearly wants to tell me all about his adventure. He talks ninety miles a minute as I get my new dress out of Maddy's car.

"Did you tell Matt thank you for such a great day?" I ask when he pauses to take a breath.

Grady's eyes widen and he turns to Matt, launching himself to tackle him in a huge hug. Matt catches him with wide arms and a light "oompf".

"Thank you, Matt! It was the best day ever!!" he yells directly into Matt's ear.

Matt laughs ruefully, "You're welcome buddy."

"Well, this has been fun. I should probably get on the road, though," Maddy announces regretfully.

I come around the car and hug her tight. "Thanks, Maddy, I had a great time. Text me later?"

"I did too!" She nods and give me a wink; she has a date this week that I definitely want to hear about.

Matt hugs his sister tightly and says goodbye. We all wave as she backs out of his driveway and pulls away.

"Mom, can we have pizza for dinner?" Grady asks as soon as Maddy is out of eyesight.

"Sure, Bud," I agree easily. Pizza nights aren't just his favorite, they're mine too.

"Can Matt come over and watch a movie with us?" Grady asks sweetly.

I glance at Matt with uncertainty. "Um, of course. Matt, Sunday nights are usually pizza and movie night. You are welcome to join us if you don't have plans," I offer.

Matt smiles. "I'd love to if I'm not intruding," he says, surprising me by accepting. This can't count as a date, right?

As a group, we walk over to my house and in through the open garage door.

"Matt! Come see my room!!" Grady calls as he shoots through the house.

"What kind of pizza do you like?" I ask as Matt follows Grady down the hall.

"I'll like whatever you like," he offers nonchalantly.

"Mom! Don't forget the cheesy bread!" Grady calls from his room.

I roll my eyes; you forget one thing one time and you never hear the end of it. I call the pizza order in and learn it'll be about forty-five minutes for delivery.

I can hear Grady speaking lightning fast, so I decide to swoop in and save Matt. "Ok guys, I ordered the pizza. Grady, you know what that means," I say pointedly.

"Aw, Mom! Not right now. I want to show Matt my Hot Wheels cars," he whines, holding up fistfuls of cars.

"You can show him after bath. Come on," I insist in my mom voice.

He looks like he is about to throw a fit, but I make my gaze sterner. I guess Grady decides getting it over with is easier than fighting about it, because he flies through his room, grabbing his pajamas and underwear before jogging to the bathroom.

I glance at Matt. "We'll just be a few minutes. Feel free to hang out in the living room or help yourself to something to drink."

"Sure," he says easily and walks back up the hall to the living room.

CHAPTER 10

Grady attempts a record-breaking bath but, given that his entire body wasn't even wet before he tried to get out and claim he was finished, I had him re-do it. He is getting more and more frustrated that I am making him take a real bath when I finally say, "Grady, if you had just done it the right way to begin with, we would be done by now." He seems put off by this but straightens up and finishes quickly without further complaint.

I towel dry his hair and comb it after he put on his pajamas, barely finishing before he shoots through the house back to Matt. I clean up the bathroom and pick up his clothes to put in the hamper before joining them.

"Mom, can we watch *Cars* tonight? Matt's never seen it," Grady asks, having already pulled out the movie.

"Sure, Buddy," I agree easily.

"And can I bring out my Hot Wheels to play with while we watch?" he presses.

"Only your Cars Hot Wheels," I counter. If he brought out all his Hot Wheels, I'd be buried under them for weeks.

Grady races to his room. "He is very excited you are here," I tell Matt unnecessarily.

Matt smiles pleasantly. "I'm happy to be here. He's a great kid."

"I hope you don't mind a Disney movie?" I ask somewhat self-consciously.

Matt smiles affectionately, then adds, "I'm definitely okay with it."

I'm not ready for the emotion contained in his gaze, so I put some distance between us. "Can I get you anything to drink?" I offer, heading to the kitchen and telling him the choices.

I pour him some lemonade and take it back into the living room while Grady drags his bag of miniature cars into the middle of the floor, excitedly telling Matt about each and every one as he takes it out.

When the doorbell rings, I spring up to get it, but Matt beats me there.

"Matt?" I ask questioningly as he pulls open the door.

"Let me treat, it's the least I can do." Without waiting for an answer, he hands the delivery guy cash. Then, he turns to me, handing me the boxes.

"You didn't have to do that," I say a little embarrassed and a little offended.

"Hey, you've fed me twice already, and you are having me over tonight. Seems like I still owe you at least one more meal," he justifies stubbornly.

I roll my eyes in irritation. "I don't think it's a tit-for-tat kind of thing but whatever."

I lay out the pizza on the kitchen counter and set out some paper plates before popping the movie in.

"Grady, let's say the blessing," I remind him, lest he just dig in like the barbarian child he wants to be.

He solemnly folds his hands together, and we start singing "God our Father," joined by Matt. We each get our plate and sit down in the living room, me on one side of the couch, Matt on the other, and Grady alternating between us and on the floor playing with his cars.

About thirty minutes before the movie ends, Grady comes to sit next to me on the couch, and just like he does every week, he snuggles up beside me, eventually laying down his head on my lap and falling asleep. When the movie finishes, Matt smiles warmly at Grady sleeping on my lap.

"Want me to carry him to his room?" he offers softly.

"I got it, thanks."

I probably should have let him, but honestly, I'm just not ready to see a man carrying my son to bed. My heart would break wide open, and that would be the end of me. I edge out from under Grady, and then pick him up, gently carrying him to bed. He's definitely hit a growth spurt because he is heavier than last week. I kiss him and tuck him in,

CHAPTER 10

turning on his night light and sound machine before closing his door softly and going back out to the living room to Matt.

To my surprise, Matt is picking up Grady's Hot Wheels and putting them back in the bag. "You don't have to do that. Grady will do it," I say as I move to the kitchen.

Matt finishes anyway, and I grab another piece of pizza and sit on the couch.

"Does he fall asleep like that every week?" Matt asks.

"Every week. He has yet to make it through a whole movie," I say in amusement.

Matt laughs, "I've never seen him so still."

"I know right? He has so much energy," I say fondly.

"Does he wake up at night?" Matt questions.

"Never. He is a really good sleeper. Honestly, I couldn't be more grateful. Mama needs her sleep!" I say, not joking in the least.

Matt settles in on the couch near me. "Tell me about your shopping trip with Maddy today."

I open my mouth but pause. "Wanna take this party outside?"

Matt smiles and follows me out to the front porch where I light the candles he gave me.

"I had the best day. I think Maddy might be my soul mate. She is hilarious. I laughed until I cried. Literally. I had tears streaming down my face. I'm sure the other people at the coffee shop thought I was a total lunatic," I say with a giggle.

Matt can't hold back his smile, which hits me in the chest just like all the others. "That's my Maddy. Always the life of the party," he says lovingly.

I look at him, happy to smile back. "She adores you, ya know. She practically idolizes you. It's really sweet."

I think I see a little pink in his cheeks even though he's trying to hide it. "She's a good sister. I adore her too." He sighs as if he's relaxing and put his arm across the back of the swing. "I'm real glad you had fun today."

"Thanks. I can't remember the last time I went out with a friend. It was more than six years ago, I can tell you that," I say with an amused huff. "Grady certainly had a blast today. Thanks for all the time you are spending with him. He couldn't be more infatuated with you," I say sincerely.

"I love Grady," Matt confesses, "He is fun." We sway for a moment before he throws out a question. "What about you?"

I look at him in confusion. "What about me?"

"Well, my sister adores me, Grady idolizes me, what about you?" he asks with a sparkle in his eye.

"Ah," I say in comprehension, buying time, "I have to say, Knight, you have quite the fan club. It's an awful lot of competition for an admirer such as myself," I tease. When I see Matt smile shyly, I continue. "I guess I'll just have to name myself official president, maybe reigning queen."

Matt laughs. "Wouldn't I be president of my own fan club?"

"Would you? I just assumed it would be a fan. I can't say I really know how it works; I've never been part of a fan club before. Maybe I'll stick with reigning queen. I know a little more about monarchy," I tease.

Matt put his hand on my shoulder and says in complete contentment, "I don't mind the sound of that."

Chapter 11

Brittany

"My, don't you look pleased," Lily says Thursday as I walk over to her treatment chair. "I've been dying to know—did you use the candles?"

I laugh when I answer, "I did. That very night." It's funny how a week ago feels like a lifetime ago.

Lily watches me expectantly. "And?"

"And every night since," I admit shyly.

She squeals, "I want to know everything. Don't hold back."

I laugh as I hook the IV to her port and start at the beginning. "...And since that weekend, I meet him every night on my front porch swing," I finish with a pleased smile.

"Are you going to ask him to go to the nurses' gala with you?" Lily asks impishly.

I stare at her in surprise. "I hadn't even thought about it. It's a work thing."

Lily continues, "So? You are getting dressed up, you have to go to an event. Why not bring a date?"

I contemplate the idea, soon aware I am nibbling on my lip. "I'm not sure I want our first date to be a gala," I say with uncertainty.

"I think it sounds romantic," Lily said dreamily.

I snort and shoot her a look. "You think everything's romantic."

Lily smiles wistfully. "I prefer to live my life with a certain...whimsy."

I laugh at Lily's unrepentant romanticism. "So how have you been?"

"Fine. Pretty normal. I get tired easily, but other than that, I'm fine," she says lightly.

"How's Joe?" I prompt.

She rolls her eyes in annoyance. "Honestly, I'm wishing for the silent treatment to return. He's hovering and needy. It's sweet, but he's driving me batty," she complains openly.

I can't help but be amused by her irritation. "He's just insecure because he is anticipating losing you."

Lily sighs in reluctant resignation. "I know. I try to be understanding of that, but...he *is* suffocating me."

"It'll get better. You'll find balance." I snap my fingers when I remember a thought I'd had earlier this week. "Hey, I meant to ask, do you and Joe want to come to Grady's birthday party in a couple weeks?" I give her the date and the details and watch her eyes light up.

"I would love to do that! What can we bring him as a gift? What does he want? Oh, Joe will have such fun picking out a gift for a little boy!" she says with Grady-level enthusiasm.

I smile, pleased; I had no idea she would get so excited. I give her a few gift ideas, then she asks conspiratorially, "Will Matt be there?"

"Actually, he will," I admit with a shy grin.

She squeals again. "I can't wait to meet him!" she says as she dances in her chair.

I clear my throat nervously, remembering the confession I need to make before she meets him. "Actually, Lil, I want to let you know that I told him about you."

"Oh." Lily's eyes dim and her face falls.

"Nothing specific, obviously. I first told him about a patient who was a family member, then he asked about you and I gave him your name. I

CHAPTER 11

shared some of what we've talked about," I clarify.

Lily nods slowly, digesting this. "Okay," she says with disappointment.

I am uncomfortable, and I can tell Lily is uncomfortable too. "He actually thinks you are pretty brave," I offer hoping to ease the situation.

"Really?" she asks, gazing at me in interest.

"I know, that's what I said." I say this with a teasing grin, then add seriously, "But he said some really sweet and touching things about your bravery to live life on your own terms and give the gift of memories to your family. It was really sweet."

"I can't wait to meet him, Britt," she says in anticipation. "He won't tell, right?" she asks in concern.

I shake my head vehemently. "No, absolutely not. He won't tell."

***

"How was your day?" Matt greets me as I sit down beside him on the swing.

As I told Lily earlier, I've met Matt on the front porch swing every night for the past couple of weeks. Through the course of the week, he has kept putting his arm on the back of the swing. Somehow, each night, I have inched closer and closer to him. It's taken a little over a week, but I am finally snuggled against his side with his arm draped down around my shoulders. Nothing's ever felt better.

"Good. I saw Lily today."

He smiles as he remembers. "Right, it's Thursday. How is she doing?"

"She's good. I invited her to Grady's birthday party, and she got so excited. She can't wait to meet you." I take a breath, "Don't forget not to say anything about her condition, though. She was pretty worried when I told her I'd told you."

"I won't say anything. That's only right," he promises.

I sigh in relief, next asking, "How was your day?"

He tells me about his work on the house. We sway and talk, sometimes falling into comfortable silence.

"So, I was thinking..." Matt starts hesitantly.

"Yeah?" I prompt.

"I was wondering if you would go on a date with me this weekend?" he asks tentatively.

I take a breath in an attempt to slow my now thundering heart. I mean, is it already time for us to leave the porch? It really hasn't been that long. Shouldn't we wait longer to...take this thing public? I'm being silly. I know I am. We have to venture out into the world at some point, right? But doesn't going out on a date make it a thing, though? Am I ready for a thing?

"Yeah, that would be nice," I say eventually, with a hint of reservation. Ready or not, here I come...I guess. If I have to.

"I didn't know if your parents would be back to watch Grady...if not, we can bring him. I don't mind," Matt offers sweetly.

I look into the eyes of the most thoughtful man I have ever known sitting next to me and go through my mental calendar. "They won't be back until the weekend of Grady's birthday party," I explain with regret.

He presents another option. "Maybe we could do dinner somewhere fun and casual, and then putt-putt or something like that?"

"That sounds great, Matt. Are you sure?" I ask self-consciously.

He brushes my arm with his hand. "Of course I am. I love hanging out with the two of you. It'll be fun."

I just don't know about this. I mean, men aren't really like this, right? They don't go on dates with single moms and their sons. I internalize my doubt and confusion to pick apart at a later time. I'll keep waiting for the other shoe to drop, because one always does. But in the meantime...I decide to take Lily's advice and not fight. That's what I'm doing here.

CHAPTER 11

I'm fighting. I should just let this happen. Besides, there's still a whole other week of porch sitting nights between now and the potential date. Feeling better by the moment, I get a little carried away. In fact, I choose to go a step further and embrace the situation.

"Actually, I was wondering...," I start and take a deep breath before my courage fails, "if you would want to maybe go with me to the nurses' gala?"

Matt smiles brilliantly. "Sure! That sounds fun," he says excitedly, and I can't tell if it's because he wants to go to the event or if he's just happy I asked him.

"It's black tie," I say almost regretfully. This will be the deal breaker I am sure.

"Not a problem," he says dismissively.

"Really?" I ask doubtfully.

He gazes at me hesitantly. "Yeah, why would it be?"

Filled with uncertainty and awkward nervousness, I blurt, "A guy that wants to take me on a date, with my son, and then go to a black-tie gala with me?" Surely, he sees the cause for my confusion.

Matt is silent for several minutes as we sway on the swing, his fingers drawing lazy circles on my arm. I am half afraid he is mad at me, but I don't know what to say.

"Did Maddy tell you I was engaged before?" he asks softly.

"She may have mentioned it," I admit vaguely.

He sits quietly in thought for another few moments. "I met her in college, was totally infatuated with her. I saw what I wanted to see, I guess. I was young and in love, or so I thought. She left me for my best friend, and it took me a long time to even look at another woman." He swivels his head and gazes at me with his clear green eyes sparkling. "Then I met you. This beautiful, loving, strong woman next door who is sweet and caring." He sighs deeply and looks straight ahead again, then turns his gaze back to me shortly. "I have fears too, Brittany. I feel vulnerable too. I am waiting for the other shoe to drop too. Wondering if I am going to screw this up, if you are going to come to your senses, or if I might traumatize Grady for life by doing something stupid."

I stare at him in utter shock. I have never even considered this from his point of view. After a moment of pause, he says, "I guess for me, though, I am willing to take the risk because Grady's a great kid. You are an amazing woman. To get the opportunity to spend time with the two of you, that's a privilege I'm not taking lightly. Just know that I'm being slow and cautious for you, but for me too."

I stare at him as he finishes, my heart bursting at the raw vulnerability in his eyes.

"Wow," I whisper quietly. "Matt, thank you for telling me that. I...." I want to share my own feelings, but I'm not sure what they are completely. I feel like I owe it to him to be honest like he is with me. "I like spending time with you. I like how you are with Grady. I like learning more about you every day, and how considerate and thoughtful you are. It's just...all new. It's all new to me. I'm willing to risk it, though, because next time Grady falls asleep on me, I want you to carry him to bed, that is if you want to. It's just that I have a little more on the line...."

"We'll figure it out together...slowly," he says with sweet reassurance. His smile widens until he chuckles to himself.

"What?"

"My plan is shaping up rather nicely. Ahead of schedule actually," he says smugly.

I laugh. "You and your plans," I say with an affectionate eye roll.

Chapter 12

Brittany

A little over a week later on Saturday evening, Matt picks us up for dinner at a local deli and a fun evening of putt-putt. The three of us have a great time, talking and laughing at Grady's antics on the putt-putt course. After we play a few rounds, with Matt and I looking past Grady's extra putts, we go inside to the arcade and take turns against Grady in different games. I follow Matt and Grady around collecting their tickets and watch some of the other mom's gaze jealously at Matt. He is incredibly handsome; I can't blame them. Somehow, him letting my son win a game of skee-ball makes him even more attractive.

He brings us home when it's close to Grady's bedtime and walks us to the door. We call a brief intermission, long enough for me to get Grady bathed and in the bed before I meet him on the porch.

Both of us still are in our date clothes when I sit down beside him. "That was fun," I say on a happy breath.

"Very fun," he agrees.

We proceed to recall our favorite moments, laughing with each other as we narrate them. After a long while of swaying and talking, Matt stands and pulls me up alongside him.

"You know, I guess it's roughly about time for this date to end," he says with soft purpose, his intention clear in his eyes as he walks me to the door.

My heart hammers and I gaze wide-eyed into his eyes, wondering if he knows what I am thinking. It appears he does because he stands in front of me calmly, gathering both my hands in his with gentle comfort. "Thank you, Brittany. I had a great time tonight," he says slowly, deliberately, giving me time to process what's about to happen.

"Thank you," I whisper back breathlessly. Can he see my pulse freaking out on my neck?

His hands drop mine and one goes to my waist, the other to my cheek as he pulls me close. "You are beautiful, do you know that?" he asks brushing his thumb across my cheek.

That's a rhetorical question, right? I stare at him and hold my breath, half scared that any movement might ruin the moment. He gazes into my eyes and leans his head down slowly. So slowly. I would have wondered what was taking so long except I am about to pass out from not breathing. I gasp when his lips touch mine gently.

My mind goes blank, my heart stops. All I can feel are his lips on mine. The kiss moves seamlessly from soft and gentle to deep and passionate without much thought. I can say with absolute certainty that, although it's been a while since I've dated, a kiss has never felt like this before. Tingles spread out through my body, starting from where our lips have touched. A wave of rightness pulls me under and holds me there, forcing me to acknowledge the undeniable truth of how well we fit together. When Matt gently pulls back, it takes me a minute to open my eyes and restart my heart. It is at this point I realized my hands are in his hair. Geez, I'm not sure how I missed that, but I'm glad I realize it because his hair is exceptionally soft. I pull my hands down and wrap my arms around his waist, hugging him close.

When I finally step back, he says affectionately, "Good night, Brittany. Sweet dreams."

CHAPTER 12

"Night, Matt," I reply simply, heart thumping and pulse thundering in my ears, wondering what in the world just happened.

* * *

"Please tell me you asked him to the gala," Lily says before I even reach her chair.

"I did," my giggle admits, "and he is coming."

"Thank God! I've been thinking about that all week. So what's going on?" she asks excitedly.

I hold out on her a little just because it's fun. "Not much. How about you?"

She pouts, chastising, "Don't play hard to get, Brittany. I don't have the patience or the life span for it."

I roll my eyes with a grin. "It's rude to keep throwing your prognosis in my face like that, you know."

"Let me have my fun," Lily grins cheekily.

I sit down beside her and tell her about the date...and the kiss. Then I share the story of Maddy's date until we were both howling with laughter. Maddy and I have been texting fairly regularly, and I was overjoyed when she called to update me about her date earlier this week.

"Oh, Brittany, this has been so much fun," Lily says breathlessly.

"Good," I say, pleased with myself. "I'm looking forward to Grady's party this weekend. That's when Matt will get to meet my parents," I say with more optimism than I feel.

Lily eyes me knowingly. "Are you nervous?"

"Sort of...yes...terrified," I admit finally in defeat.

Lily giggles, "Why?"

"I don't know. My dad has been the only man in mine and Grady's life for so long. My parents have been close to Grady, keeping him for me and everything. I just...I don't want them to feel threatened," I rush out with great anxiety.

Lily laughs outright. Full out, and long.

"I'm getting really tired of you laughing at my legitimate concerns," I grumble.

"Those aren't legitimate concerns. It's fear, plain and simple. When you show him off to your parents, it's real. It's not just something on your front porch in the dark anymore. You are really doing this."

I eye her. I hate that she is so stinking perceptive. It's incredibly annoying.

"Bite the bullet, Britt. You're good," she says confidently.

I huff in annoyance. "Easy for you to say."

She shrugs unconcerned. "Maybe, but you'll be glad once it's over."

"Why do you say that?" I ask curiously.

"Because right now you are standing at the edge, about to take the leap. No one wants to leap. It's scary and it's a long way down. Once you're down there, though, you realize it's exactly where you want to be," Lily says serenely.

I take in her words and hope to God they are true. "You talk like you're ninety-five years old you know," I tease with an amused smirk.

She admits, "Joe and my parents say I'm an old soul." She pauses and deflates a little. "Plus, I think it's true that dying does give you perspective."

I take her hand. "You're not dead yet, Lil."

She smiles at me. "You know, I will forever be grateful that our renewed friendship is a byproduct of this incredibly sad thing." She tilts her head and looks at me strangely, saying, "I guess that's what God does, He makes beauty from ashes."

I think about her words all day. They keep rolling around in my head, and when I pick Grady up from day camp, I realize, whether she meant

CHAPTER 12

to or not, she was also referring to my son.

It's true. God took this awful, hurtful, painful thing in my life and made something beautiful with it. The most encouraging thing is He may not be done.

Chapter 13

Brittany

The day of Grady's birthday party he is practically vibrating he is so excited. I must have heard thirty thousand times, "Mom, is it time yet?" Finally, with great relief, I tell him yes, it is time. We meet Matt in front of the house and walk over to Gran and Pop's house together, with Grady riding his bike out in front of us.

"Are you nervous?" Matt asks me as we walk.

I look up at him and admit in a small voice, "A little. You?"

"A little," he grins reassuringly.

I laugh as I hear Grady screaming in joy, "Gran! Pop! You're back!"

"Oh gosh, the whole neighborhood knows now," I say in amusement.

"Has he been like this all day?" Matt asks, curiously. I can't tell if he's impressed that Grady's excitement can top what he's already seen so far or worried.

"Pretty much since yesterday," I confirm.

I wave to my parents as we approach, noting how both my mom and dad are standing and watching us walk together. I had, of course, told my parents about Matt and explained he was coming today. They are, understandably, very anxious to meet him.

"Hi Mom, Dad! Good to have you home," I say, giving them each a

CHAPTER 13

hug.

"Only for the week, love. The ocean air is calling my name," Mom says wistfully.

"Mom, Dad, this is Matt Knight, our next-door neighbor and a good friend of Grady's and mine," I say introducing him.

"Nice to meet you, Matt. We've heard such wonderful things about you. From Brittany and from Grady," Mom says pleasantly with an observational eye.

"Pop! Pop! Please come in the pool with me now, please!" Grady begs, running around us in circles.

"Come on, Grady boy, let's go and let Gran get acquainted with Matt," Dad says eyeing Matt warily.

I smile in apology to Matt.

"Brittany, honey, would you start the grill? Matt, you come help me in the kitchen," Mom instructs.

"But Mom..." I start to protest.

"Thank you, Brittany, you know where the lighter is," Mom says, taking Matt's arm and leading him into the house without allowing further discussion.

Geez, I didn't know they were going to completely remove him from my presence. I watch Grady and Dad play in the pool as I start the grill.

"What's up, Short Stuff?" I hear and feel a pinch.

I jump and squeal, turning on the perpetrator. "Derek! That hurt!"

He laughs. "Come on, that was nothing."

"I thought you were on duty today," I said grudgingly, rubbing my arm where he pinched me.

"Dad called. Said you had a boyfriend," he says, scanning the backyard.

"Derek, don't you dare say anything to him," I warn.

He winks with a huge grin. "I'm going to say all kinds of things to him. Where is he?"

I don't answer, but I catch my Dad pointing to the kitchen. I roll my eyes; there is officially a conspiracy going on.

Mom brings out the meat and I try to question her, but she perfectly times her drop off with the arrival of a group of Grady's friends, slipping to me and away without a word. Before I know it, I'm talking to mothers and manning the grill at the same time, multitasking like a boss. The smell of chlorine from the pool mixes with the smell of cooking meat from the grill and the two combined produce a scent uniquely summer.

"Alison!!" Grady cries in utter rapture, running out of the pool. I groan. Here we go.

Alison is a cute, little blonde girl with freckles and glasses being led in by her father, a relatively handsome, although severe-looking man.

"Hi, Gordon?" I ask. He nods and I say, "I'm Brittany. Nice to meet you."

Grady has already coerced Alison into the pool, so I lead Gordon back to the grill so I can keep an eye on the meat.

"So, that's Grady," he says, somewhat displeased.

"And Alison," I say in the same tone.

We look at each other and laugh.

"Nice to meet you in person, Brittany," he says eyeing me closely.

I nod in admission. "You too. The other parents dropped off their kids, but you can stay if you want. Up to you." I kind of hope he leaves because he makes me nervous, but he doesn't know me and I wouldn't let Grady stay somewhere where I didn't know the people. Especially at a pool party.

"I'll stay, thanks. So community center day camp, right?" he asks.

"Yeah, that's right," I confirm.

"Alison tried to talk me into switching her," Gordon mumbles in displeasure.

Amused at their antics, I chuckle. "Grady tried the same with the Y. His other friends were at the community center, though."

CHAPTER 13

"Same for Alison," Gordon agrees.

"It can't be a crush, right? Aren't they are still too young for that?" I ask, gazing at the two of them playing in the pool. Grady has officially forsaken all his other friends, all his attention on Alison.

"Of course they are. It's harmless. They're friends," he adds, but he doesn't sound certain as he watches them too.

"We are in big trouble," I say in resignation.

"Yup," he agrees miserably and we both laugh.

"Need any help, babe?" Matt asks as he puts his arm around my shoulders and stands between me and Gordon. I'm a little surprised because we haven't gotten to pet names and public displays of affection yet, but the pleasure I get from feeling his arm around me, pressed into his side, gives me a face-splitting grin despite my surprise.

I smile up at him and answer back, "Nope, I'm good."

He introduces himself to Gordon, and then gets in the pool to play with Grady and his friends.

"Boyfriend?" Gordon asks, watching Matt curiously.

"Yes," I say absently, flipping burgers, but then I rethink my answer. Is Matt my boyfriend? Is this an official conversation admission or just like an understood thing? I wonder at the appropriate ratio for nights on a porch swing to dates to being someone's girlfriend.

Gordon nods. "Grady like him?"

I watch as Grady launches himself playfully at Matt. "Oh yeah."

Gordon clears his throat and goes on, "That's good. Alison, she didn't like my last...girlfriend."

I glance at him and he looks conflicted. I don't know what to say. "I've never really dated, until Matt. So I don't really have any experience with all this," I admit.

Gordon eyes me in surprise, then looks back at Matt. "Lucky," he murmurs.

"Yeah, I am," I say with pleasure.

He smirks and looks at me, confirming, "Yeah, you too." I'm distracted from questioning his response by someone calling my name.

"Brittany! Hey!" I look over and see Lily and her husband, Joe, coming over.

"Lily! It's great to see you!" I greet. Mom comes over to welcome Lily and her husband and catch up.

"Hey, party people!" Maddy cries out as she walks through the gate.

I walk over and hug her. "Thanks for coming, Maddy. Grady is so excited to see you again."

"Wouldn't miss it," she beams. "Mom and Dad are a little put out they weren't invited, but I promised them pics. It's too soon," she says with an understanding nod.

"Too soon," I nod. No way am I ready for that.

"Maddy!!" Grady calls as he runs from the pool and hugs her legs... sopping wet.

I mouth to her "sorry." She just laughs and hugs him back. Maddy is in a colorful summer dress and designer sandals; she looks like a model. I am momentarily jealous, until I see Matt gazing at me from the pool. Suddenly, I feel better about my mom bun, tank top, and shorts. It's too stifling out today, particularly by the grill, to be too concerned with being fashionable. I introduce Maddy around, and she quickly discards her dress revealing her flattering but fairly modest two-piece swimsuit. I thought I saw Derek's gaze linger over her when they met, but I chuckle when he near about swallows his tongue seeing her in that swimsuit.

Grady and his friends play in the pool until the food is ready, and by ready I mean a little over done because I was chatting with Lily and Mom instead of watching the food.

"Okay everybody, lunch!" I call over the talking adults and the children's squeals coming from the pool.

Dad, Derek, Maddy, and Matt herd the kids out of the pool while Mom and I help each one make a plate and find a seat. Once the kids have all eaten, we bring out the cake and sing to Grady. I'm not gonna lie, I tear up a little. Seven. He's seven.

The kids have cake, then we do presents, and I hold my breath until Grady says thank you after each gift like we discussed at length this morning. By the time he is finished, the kids' food has properly settled, and we let them all back into the pool, supervised by Matt, Derek, Maddy, and Dad, who take turns throwing them around and playing with them in the water.

The rest of us sit on the patio, chatting under an umbrella and watching the kids play. I have no idea how much time passes, but it's been at least an hour and a half when I hear my mom talking about reapplying sunscreen.

"Lily?" Joe prompts quietly.

I smile without looking at them. Joe is indeed very attentive to Lily. He has hovered and worried over her all day. Surprisingly, she says, "Yes, I guess we should be going." She stands and gives me a big hug. "Thank you for inviting us, Brittany."

I hug her back, then my Mom grabs a hug too. "So good to catch up with you, dear. Don't be a stranger now."

Lily waves to everyone in the pool before leaving. Soon after she leaves, some of the moms arrive to pick up their kids. The guests start to leave, and Grady thanks them each for coming, giving them a bag of candy as a party favor. I'm so proud of his manners.

"Aren't you a proud mama bear," Matt says with a smile, coming to stand next to me.

"Of course. He's been the perfect gentleman," I say proudly.

Once the kids have left, including Alison and her dad, Mom and I get in the pool to play with Grady. The cool water is a welcome relief after hostess duties in the sweltering heat. I wear my modest one-piece today, but I can't help but feel Matt's eyes lingering on me, and I like it.

"Mom! Watch!" Grady calls. I smile because he must say that a million times when we are at my parents' pool. I relax on the steps in the shallow end and watch him, allowing the refreshing water to wash away the remaining stress from the party.

"I like him. I'll let you know what the background check says, but my gut says he's good," Derek says in a voice for me only as he comes to sit beside me.

"Don't you dare," I warn as menacingly as I can.

"I'll run his plates too. Just to double check," he says with a grin.

"You are so annoying," I mutter. "Thanks for coming today, though. Grady adores you, ya know. You could come by more often," I suggest. This is not the first time I've scolded him for this offence.

He actually looks pained this time. "I know. I'm sorry. Seven. I mean, geez, I missed his whole childhood."

I nod silently because he did.

"I just..." he sighs, "I don't know, Britt. I just couldn't deal after what happened to you. It wasn't fair. There wasn't justice... I couldn't protect you...I guess I just..." he stops short.

I am shocked. I had no idea it had anything to do with that. I thought he was just busy. I mean I knew he was going through some stuff, but I didn't know it had to do with me. I put my hand on his arm. "I love you Derek, and Grady loves you. We would love to see you whenever you have the time," I say simply.

After a moment or two of silence, I look over and confirm my suspicion. He is watching Maddy. "Do I detect a little interest in you, bro?"

Derek glares at me with his detective's face. I laugh as I tease, "You can't pull that on me. I know you, and I know that look!" I say pointing at him.

"Leave it, Short Stuff," he says warningly.

I laugh again, enjoying him squirm. "Don't like it when you're the one in the hot seat, huh?"

He frowns. "Whatever. She's not even from here," he says more to himself than to me.

"It's a short drive," I suggest meaningfully.

My brother only eyes me behind his sunglasses.

I turn back to watch Grady, a smile on my lips, when I notice Maddy glancing over at Derek repeatedly.

"Well, well, looks like your interest is reciprocated," I grin slyly at him. "This should be fun."

With a snort, he gets up out of the pool. "Well, I need to get going, actually. I traded for a night shift."

"Come on!" I huff, "Don't leave yet."

"Duty calls," he replies, unaffected by my protests.

Grady comes over to give him a hug, and Matt shakes his hand before Derek leaves. I definitely notice disappointment on Maddy's face when he goes. We stay another hour because I want Grady good and tired before we head home.

To make it simple, we eat leftovers from lunch for dinner before Maddy announces she should head to their parents' house. I hug her, and so does Grady, and she promises to stop by before leaving town the next day.

A few minutes later, Grady rides his bike while my dad drives Matt and I home in his golf cart, hauling the gifts and leftovers home for us.

"Thanks, Daddy," I say, kissing his cheek before he goes.

He grunts and says, "Yard looks good."

I beam because I know that's the closest he's gonna get to telling me he likes Matt.

"Mom, can Matt come over for a movie?" Grady pleads.

"Sure, Buddy. Bath first," I say firmly.

"One for me too," Matt says with a grin.

"Just come in when you're ready. I'll leave the front door open." I say with a smile.

I take Grady to the tub and, though he has calmed considerably, he is still very excited. I smile because I know the movie will put him to sleep.

"Mom?" he says during his bath.

"Mhmm," I say while washing his hair.

"Is Matt gonna be my daddy?"

I pause and consider my words carefully. "I don't know. Buddy. Do you want him to be?"

I take my sudsy hands out of his hair and watch his brown eyes turn round. "Yeah, I do. Is that okay?"

I take a deep breath before saying, "Well, you know Matt and I are friends. I don't know what's gonna happen yet." I say it carefully, but I can tell he doesn't understand. "Let's just focus on being friends with Matt right now. Okay, Buddy? We can just be friends with him for now, right?" I ask hopefully.

Although I can tell he isn't completely satisfied, he nods and I breathe a sigh in relief. We finish his bath and he immediately surrounds himself with every single gift he got today on the floor of the living room.

Matt comes in and grins at the scene. "He looks happy."

I smirk, replying "You could say that."

We pop in the movie Grady says he wants to watch, and this time Matt is not on the opposite end of the couch. I'm leaning against him with his arm behind me and my legs curled underneath me. It only takes about an hour for Grady to fall asleep watching the movie, but we don't move him. Instead, I lean more and more on Matt until my head is resting on his shoulder. Such a strong shoulder.

Eventually, my pillow moves and I stir, not realizing I have been asleep. "Sorry to wake you, but the movie is over."

I nod sleepily, coming into awareness. "Can you get Grady for me?" He nods and gingerly picks him up, carrying Grady to his bed.

CHAPTER 13

That picture will rest in my heart for all of eternity.

I follow and turn on my son's nightlight, tuck him in, and start his sound machine. I kiss Grady and pray over him, then I follow Matt out the door, closing it gently.

I head back to the couch and reach for Matt, who is right behind me, promptly trying to find the same position I was in earlier.

"Brittany?" he says gently against my hair.

"Hmm?"

"Today was a great day. Thanks for including me and Maddy," he says sincerely.

I giggle before returning, "I'll ask you how you feel about that after Derek and Maddy eventually start dating."

"What?" he asks in surprise.

I lean back and look at him with a mischievous grin. "Oh yeah. Get ready."

Matt looks thoughtful at the new situation. "Well, well, I guess I'm not the only one who's getting a background check."

I groan. "I'm so sorry. Were they awful? I had no idea my parents were going to separate us."

"They were fine," he smiles. "They love you and Grady an awful lot."

"Yeah," I say with a satisfaction, "They do."

"I think even your Dad cracked a smile," he says proudly.

"I know he did. He's never ever complimented my yard before."

Matt's chest puffs out a little more at that.

"So what do you think of Alison and her dad now?" Matt asks.

I muddle over my opinions. "She's okay, I guess. I'm still not crazy about her. Gordon's nice enough I guess."

Matt is silent for a few minutes. "Nice enough, huh. That's it?"

I lean back to look at him again, questioning, "What do you mean?"

"He looked pretty interested in you from where I was sitting," Matt states matter of fact.

Gordon's comments came rushing back and I finally understand what he meant.

"Ah," I hum, snuggling into Matt a little more. "I told him you were my boyfriend."

"Good." Matt squeezed my shoulders.

I guess we have made the swing/date/boyfriend ratio.

Chapter 14

Matt

"You know Mom and Dad are getting restless. They want to meet Brittany and Grady," Maddy whispers, leaning close before the start of Sunday service.

I groan knowing she's right. "Maddy, hold them off. I'm taking this slow. Uber slow. It's amazing she even invited us to his birthday party." Maddy looks at me with sympathy. "Help me, Mads. I don't want to blow this by going too fast. We just did her parents. Let's let things settle a minute before another 'meet the parents.'"

To my great relief, Maddy nods. "Send me the picture of you two fishing. That should hold them off a little longer. I'll try explaining to Mom again."

I squeeze her hand, whispering back, "Thanks, Mads." Then I remember my reason for cornering her. "So, what's with you and Derek?"

Maddy turns large, round eyes to me and says, too innocently, "What do you mean?"

"Come on. Everyone saw you circling each other like cats in heat, Maddy," I say obviously.

She blushes deep red. "They did not. I do not circle," she hisses in haughty outrage.

I stare at her knowingly.

She cracks, just a little. "I noticed him, if that's what you mean. I'm not even sure we spoke directly to each other, though."

I keep staring.

"Fine, we talked, but he didn't even ask for my number," she huffs.

I watch her closely. Is she disappointed?

"You okay, Mads?" I ask in concern.

"I'm fine," she says brusquely, then she sighs, "I'm thinking about coming home."

"What? I thought you loved Atlanta?" I ask in surprise.

"I did. I'm a little tired of the scene now, though. Don't tell Mom and Dad. I haven't decided yet, and no way am I moving back in with them," she says sternly.

"Whatever you need, Mads, you know I'm here. You can stay with me if you want," I offer.

She smiles at me and mouths "thanks" as the service starts and our conversation is effectively cut off.

*　*　*

After lunch with my family, I drive home, Maddy following so she can say goodbye to Brittany and Grady. I have to admit, seeing those two everyday makes each day worth it. I couldn't be happier with how things are progressing. When I pull up to my house, I notice a motorcycle parked on the street near my neighbor's house, and my gut clenches. I don't know anyone who drives a motorcycle.

Maddy gets out right behind me and watches me curiously as she follows me over to the house. I knock on the door and am immediately calmed by a beaming Brittany.

CHAPTER 14

"Hey, guys! Come on in! Grady's just playing with Derek," she greets cheerfully.

I smile in relief. It's just Derek. I look at Maddy beside me and she is glancing nervously around. This should be fun.

"Matt! Maddy!" Grady calls as he launches himself at me.

I love it when he does that.

"Hey, Buddy. Playing with all your cool, new stuff?" I ask him with a smile.

"Yeah! Come see! Uncle Derek helped me build a robot," he says proudly.

I carry Grady to his room and find Derek sitting in the middle of it, playing with a robot.

I look behind me, but Maddy isn't following, so I greet Derek and join the game.

Brittany's laughter floats to me, and I look at the door just in time to see her pop her head around the corner. "Who wants birthday cake?" she calls cheerily.

"Me!" Grady yells and runs to be first to get a slice.

As Derek and I get up, I eye him. "So, am I gonna need to do a background check on you soon?" I ask, referencing our little chat in his mother's kitchen.

Derek crosses his arms over his chest and looks me up and down. "I don't know. Maybe."

He's fit, but shorter than me. I could take him if I had to, but I don't think I'll have to. Plus, although I could take him, I don't think I'd win. "If you don't know, then maybe don't go there," I say in warning, mirroring his stance. I don't want Maddy being toyed with.

Derek's gaze falters for a split second, then hardens. "Be a problem if I went there?" he asks roughly.

I take my time sizing him up, only because that's what he did to me yesterday and it's nice that the tables have turned.

"You hurt her and there'll be a problem," I say with certainty.

He narrows his gaze and stares me down. I stare back, unblinking.

"Uh, guys?" Brittany asks hesitantly from the door, looking from Derek to me and back again.

I look over at her and smile. "We're coming." Reaching to put my arm around her shoulders and follow her out, I look back and give Derek a final warning glare.

I keep my eyes on Derek and Maddy awkwardly interacting with each other in the kitchen until Brittany elbows me in the stomach.

"What's with you?" she asks.

I'm not sure how to put into words what I'm thinking, and I don't want her to get mad that I'm nervous about her brother and my sister.

"They'll be fine," she whispers, guessing at my predicament. She gives me a reassuring kiss on my cheek.

I can't help but smile when I look down at her.

"Hate to break up the party, but I gotta get home," Maddy says, kissing the top of Grady's head and then moving to hug Brittany.

I hug and kiss my sister, telling her to call me when she gets home, and she agrees.

"I'll walk you out. I should get going too," Derek says.

I move to follow, but Brittany tugs on my sleeve and shakes her head, smiling at me. "Know what?" she asks me.

"What?"

"I don't think I've ever been so excited for movie night."

I grin and pull her into a hug, forgetting about Derek and Maddy.

Chapter 15

Brittany

When I see Lily arrive, I finish with my patient as quickly as possible to get over to her.

"So," she asks with a sly smile, "How is it on the other side of the ledge?"

"Pretty amazing, I have to admit"

Lily giggles. "I told you so. Tell me," she demands.

I hook up today's treatment to her port and sit down, telling her about after the party and the past week.

"All three of us have been swimming at my parents' house almost every night this week, and then, after Grady goes to bed, Matt and I sit out on the porch," I say proudly.

Lily giggles helplessly. "I love this so much. So what do you talk about?"

I think back to our conversations, happy to share. "Everything. He always starts by asking about my day. Then we go from there, from what he is doing with his house to favorite childhood memories."

Lily eyes me. "Be honest, you make out, don't you?" she accuses playfully.

I laugh. "There is sometimes a goodnight kiss involved," I admit chastely.

Lily looks disgusted. "A goodnight kiss? That's it?"

"Behave," I say as I playfully hit her arm

She faces me appreciatively. "It's going well, huh?"

I smile. Wide. I can't help it. "Yeah."

A sly smile crosses her face. "Any chance you could hurry it up? I'd love to go to the wedding before I die."

My mouth falls open in shock and amusement. "Lily!"

"I'm just saying," she shrugs unrepentantly.

* * *

I have to say, sitting on the front porch swing in the candlelight, moon rising high, with Matt's arm around me is my happy place. In the past weeks, I've inched my way so close to him I'm almost welded against his side.

"How is Lily?" he asks.

I smile. I love that he remembers her every Thursday.

"She's good. She likes you. Wants to know if we can hurry it up so she can attend a wedding before she dies," I finish with a chuckle.

"Works for me." he says squeezing my shoulder.

I know he's kidding, so I don't respond.

"I meant to tell you, Grady and I are meeting my parents at the beach in about three weeks. We will be gone the last week in July."

Matt acknowledges this but looks disappointed. "Okay, thanks for letting me know. You go on vacation with them every year?"

I continue, "Yeah. They spend most of the summer at their beach house. Derek and I meet them there the last week in July to have a family vacation before school starts."

"That's nice. Good family time. I'll miss you though," he says with a

CHAPTER 15

frown.

"I'll miss you too," I say truthfully. "But we can still talk on the phone and text," I offer.

Matt kisses my temple and tells me, "It's not the same as holding you."

I blush. I don't know why I blush so often around him.

We sit in silence for a minute before I jump up. "Oh! I almost forgot!" I blurt and then run into the house.

I return offering him a plate. "S'mores brownies. Thank you for cutting my yard again," I say with appreciation, sitting down beside him again.

He kisses my temple again (I really love it when he does that—makes my stomach flip every time) and says, "You're welcome. You know you don't have to keep baking me treats. I would do it anyway."

"I know, but I like showing my appreciation," I say with a proud smile.

"I don't want to add more to your plate, though. Besides," he teases, "I can think of other ways for you to show your appreciation."

"Behave," I admonish, but I kiss him anyway. His kisses are so sweet and gentle that I dream about them sometimes.

"You excited about our date tomorrow night?" he asks me.

"The gala? Yes. I mean, it's just a work thing, but I'm glad I'm going with you." I say laying my head on his shoulder. "Thanks for doing that by the way."

"What are you doing Saturday? Grady's spending the night with your parents, right?" Matt asks curiously.

"Yeah. I'll probably sleep late and then head over mid-morning to swim with him. Wanna come?" I don't hesitate to offer.

He doesn't miss a beat either. "Absolutely."

I lay my head back on his shoulder and sigh in contentment. It's getting harder and harder to leave him at night.

"Me too," he rumbles.

Geez. I squeeze my eyes shut; I can't believe I said that out loud.

"When do you go back to school?" I ask, making conversation.

"First week of August. Gotta get my room ready and stuff like that. Meetings and official prep start the next week," he shares.

"Do you hate going back after the summer?" I ask curiously. I would after having all that time off.

His head tilts each way as he wavers. "I don't hate my job. I certainly don't mind going back to teach the kids, but...it's work too, you know?" I can hear the grin in his voice. "What do you do with Grady during the school year, after school I mean?" he asks curiously.

"After school care. Sometimes my Mom picks him up. He likes after care though because his friends are there," I explain easily.

We sit companionably for a few minutes.

"I could help out, if you'd like," he suggests tentatively, "Pick him up if you need someone."

I put my hand on his leg. "Thank you, Matt." I know, however, I'll never impose on him like that.

We swing until my eyelids start to droop, but I still don't want to leave him.

He gently shakes my shoulder and says, "Time for bed, sweet girl."

I grumble and inch closer, and he chuckles with tenderness. Getting up, he pulls me to my feet. "See you tomorrow. Sweet dreams."

It's the goodnight kisses that make my dreams sweet. Sometimes they're soft and gentle, other times they're demanding and passionate, but each time my heart races and my stomach dives and I'm not entirely sure how I get in the house after each one.

Chapter 16

Brittany

"Please tell me you can see this," I say on video chat with Maddy.

"Umm...sort of, but it would have been easier if I had known so I could come and help myself," she mutters grumpily.

"You were just here. You wanna come home every weekend?" I challenge.

Maddy stays silent and a blush tinges her cheeks.

"Speaking of Derek, how are things going?" I openly pry.

"We weren't speaking of Derek, and...I don't know. Can you do a smoky eye? I think that would go well with the dress."

I look at her pointedly on the screen. "I'm standing in my bathroom in my underwear on video chat with you so you can walk me through hair and makeup. What part of this entire situation makes you think I know how to do a smoky eye?"

She frowns in good humor. "Right. Okay, grasshopper, follow my instructions very carefully."

An hour and a half later, we ditch the smoky eye after three failed attempts and go with a more subtle brown shading. My makeup is done, and my arms are tired from twisting and clipping hair pieces following Maddy's specific instructions. I pull my dress on, slip on some strappy heels, and reveal the results to Maddy.

She squeals. "Oh, Brittany! You look so good. Matt's gonna flip when he sees you."

Just then, my doorbell rings.

"Speak of the devil. Thanks, Mads. You're the best!" I say quickly and hit the end chat button. I grab my clutch and rush to the front door, swinging it open.

I am not prepared for Matt in a tux. I'm not sure anything could have prepared me for Matt in a tux. Not Matt in shorts and a t-shirt, not Matt with no shirt on, not even Matt in dress pants and a polo for church. Trust me, he rocks each of those like nobody's business. Matt in a tux is... well...overwhelming.

I finally realize I'm staring him up and down, and he is staring me up and down, and neither of us has said anything. I giggle, "Perfect timing."

"Brittany, you look..." he says with something I like to think is awe in his voice. Unfortunately, he doesn't finish the sentence. He pulls me in for a kiss, and it's not a sweet and gentle one. When he pulls back, I realize the music in my head while we kissed is actually his phone ringing over and over again.

After seeing the caller, he picks up and launches into the conversation. "You are so annoying," he says emphatically. "Yes, I know. I'll do it right now. Fine, don't call again...either of us," he finishes with a warning.

I look at him questioningly, and he looks annoyed but amused at the same time. "Maddy is threatening my life if I don't get a picture before we go. Do you mind?" He holds me close and holds up his camera for a quick snap.

"Send me that, please. Oh hey, I have an idea." I walk to the kitchen to get the stand I put my phone in when I'm cooking. I prop his phone on it and put it on a timer.

CHAPTER 16

"Prom pose," I call cheekily as we get a full-length photo.

He kisses me again before retrieving his phone and sending the pics to Maddy and me. Then he takes my hand and leads me out to his truck. He helps me in and makes sure my dress isn't in the way before he shuts the door for me. I don't know if this is just a special occasion thing, but I've never known a guy who still does gentlemanly things like that. Something in the cab catches my eye as he walks around to the driver's side.

"You have a booster seat?" I ask in confusion.

He looks at me blankly. "Yeah, so I can take Grady if I need to."

I search my memory. I don't remember him taking Grady anywhere. "When did you get that?"

"After you went shopping with my sister and left your car with the booster in it in case I needed it in an emergency. I went out and got one the next day," he says nonchalantly.

I don't know why, and God knows Maddy would kill me if she knew my makeup was threatened in any way, but my eyes tear up. I take his hand and intertwine our fingers as he drives us downtown.

The event is being held in the ballroom of a swanky hotel. We walk into the event from the parking garage, and I give my name at the registration table. We survey the room as we enter, band and dance floor to one side, tables with guests sparsely gathered around to the other side, and tables lined with food along the far wall.

I scan the room until I find the other managers from my unit. I take Matt's hand and lead him over to the table, introduce him around, and try not to laugh at their open-mouthed appraisals. Matt promptly joins the other husbands and boyfriends in getting us some punch.

"Brittany!" Theresa gasps.

"I know, right," I say smugly.

We all laugh and watch Matt walk away until I hear my name behind me.

"Brittany, fancy seeing you here," says a somewhat familiar voice behind me.

I turn around and see Gordon, Alison's father. "Hi, Gordon. What a surprise." I stop myself just short of asking "what are you doing here."

His eyes light in amusement, probably reading my mind. "I'm in hospital administration."

"Ah," I say in surprise. He glances behind me and nods to my friends, shaking hands all around.

"Mr. McKay," they each greet him formally.

I didn't know his last name was McKay. McKay. Gordon McKay. The Chief Operating Officer? My eyes widen in shock.

Gordon notices the look in my eyes. "Ah, I see you've placed the name."

I blush and glance around. I've heard terrible things about him. How stern he is, yelling and firing people even when it wasn't their fault. He runs a tight ship, that's for certain.

"Brittany, would you care to dance?" Gordon asks me invitingly.

My mouth falls open. "Uh" slips out in a somewhat un-lady like fashion before I feel an arm slip around my waist.

"Gordon, great to see you," Matt says stiffly, shaking his hand. It does not go unnoticed by me that Matt came back without punch.

Gordon's face stiffens into a plastered smile. "Matt, good to see you. Another time, Brittany," he says curtly, nodding at Matt before quickly walking away.

I watch him go with eyes still wide before turning to Matt to see him grinning proudly. He kisses my lips and murmurs, "Can't leave you alone for two minutes."

I sputter, still in shock, and turn back to the group, who are watching the show in surprised amusement.

"How do you know Mr. McKay, Brittany?" Glenda asks curiously.

I find my voice. "His daughter was in the same class as my son last year. I don't really know him; I just met him when he brought his daughter to my son's birthday party."

"He seems to like you," one of them mutters.

I wrap my arm around Matt and look up at him. "Wanna grab that drink?"

He understands immediately, winking as he presents his arm gallantly. Waving to my friends, we walk toward the bar.

"Sorry," I murmur.

"Don't be," he smiles. "Apparently, I have the hottest date tonight. Of course, I was already aware of that, but it doesn't hurt to be noticed by the big wigs," he says with amusement, nodding over to where Gordon stands, watching us.

"I only want to be noticed by you tonight," I say honestly, ignoring Gordon.

Matt smiles down at me and kisses me lightly on the lips. He hands me a drink, and we mingle with other staff members of the Cancer Center. We sit down for the brief program, which is basically a few speeches detailing the importance of nurses and how appreciative the hospital administration is of us.

When the program ends, Matt leans close to my ear, kissing it softly before asking, "Hungry or do you want to dance?"

Following the program, they dim the lights and focus on the dance floor, letting the real party begin. The speakers for the band are turned up, and the musicians switch from staid background music to party music.

I look into his eyes and get lost for a moment. "Food" is all I get out.

Matt smiles devastatingly at me before taking my hand and leading me to the food tables. We proceed down the line, adding food to our plates until Matt gets caught in conversation with one of the other husbands who happens to be a coach at his school. I scan the buffet tables, trying to get enough for both of us while he talks so we can sit back down for another few minutes.

"Hungry?" I hear an amused voice ask behind me.

I look up to see Gordon again. My stomach drops uncomfortably, but I return the question in the same tone. "Matt got caught up, so I'm getting enough for two," I explain, gesturing with my head behind us.

Gordon nods. "Alison had a lot of fun at Grady's birthday party. I suppose he's an okay kid," he admits teasingly.

"I suppose Alison's pretty okay too," I respond in kind. "I'm glad she had fun."

I move further down the tables, Gordon following. "I was thinking maybe we could set a playdate or something together in the next few weeks. I know Alison would really like to see Grady again."

I hesitate, but tentatively agree. "Yeah, maybe. You have my number. So if you have a free day text me," I say lightly.

I glance toward Matt, but he is in deep conversation. Gordon is watching me closely and getting a little too much into my personal space, increasing my discomfort.

"I'll do that," Gordon says with a creepy gleam in his eye.

"For a playdate," I clarify. "For the kids."

He nods, his gleam dimming but still there. "Of course," he says like a gentleman.

I smile politely and leave the buffet, only having gone down halfway before placing myself firmly next to Matt. It is reassuring when I feel his arm go around my waist. I don't look back toward Gordon, but I am relieved when I don't feel his eyes on me anymore. Matt leads me to our table and helps me with my chair.

"Sorry I left you, but if I didn't, he would've kept following you around until he had his moment," Matt explains.

"He wants to setup a play date for the kids," I say, watching Matt closely.

"I would be happy to handle that if you need me to," he offers with a

CHAPTER 16

grin.

I laugh at his implication. "I don't know why, but he kind of gives me the creeps."

Matt winks. "Good, can't have my girl going on playdates with guys she likes."

I laugh again. We comfortably settle in to eating and chatting with the other couples at our table. When we finish, we moved around the room, mingling a little more before the band plays a slow song.

Matt tugs me toward the dance floor. "Come on, let's dance."

I can't help enjoy my happy smile as I follow him onto the floor and am swept up into his arms, reveling in his strength.

"I hope you are okay with the middle school shuffle back and forth. I don't really know how to dance," I confess with a self-conscious laugh.

He smiles down at me, holding me tighter. "Just follow my lead."

He spins us around with a flourish and I laugh again, enjoying Matt's excitement. He looks into my eyes and appears...smug.

"What?" I say at his expression.

"Can you blame me for wanting to show off the most beautiful woman in the room tonight?" Matt says playfully.

I tilt my head in amusement. "My, aren't we laying it on a little thick," I tease.

Matt grows serious. "Nope, cold hard truth. I love you, Brittany."

I smile softly as we sway on the dance floor while he holds me close to his chest. His perfect green eyes stare into mine, begging for me to respond with the same. Should I be surprised at what he said? I'm not at all. I'm a little surprised he admitted his love right here, now, but I'm not surprised at all that's how he feels. I'm not sure I've thought all that much about being in love with him, I've been so consumed with worry and doubt, but that's what has happened. All those nights on the porch have led to this. I've fallen in love with him.

"I love you too, Matt," I say quietly, more startled that I've admitted the truth to myself much less to him. I still worry; I still doubt. There is a lot to figure out for our future, but I can't deny that I love him.

His smile is brilliant. My shy smile peeks through after he tugs me a little closer.

"I already knew, but it's nice to hear all the same," he says teasingly.

"Oh, did you? Getting a little cocky, don't you think?" I tease right back.

"Only for you, baby," he finishes, twirling me around one last time as the song ends.

***

Matt

The only thing that would make tonight more perfect is if Gordon would stop staring at us. I'm roundly ignoring him but can't help but notice he keeps showing up in my peripheral vision, eyes fixed on us. Well, one of us more than the other.

"I'm ready, are you?" Brittany asks me.

I answer, "Whenever you are."

Brittany leads us back to tell her coworkers goodbye, and I work on shielding Brittany from Gordon.

Unfortunately, he intercepts us on our way out the door, invading Brittany's personal space. I put my arm protectively around her, tugging my girl close.

"Leaving so soon?" Gordon asks. He wobbles a little and his speech sounds slurred. I did notice before that he'd been drinking quite a bit.

"We are heading home," Brittany says politely.

"I'll call you," Gordon promises to Brittany, practically leering at her. His gaze flicks to me, and I glower at him.

"About the playdate, for the kids," Brittany states stiffly. "You can

CHAPTER 16

always text me." She tugs me past him quickly, and I am grateful because this guy is really starting to piss me off.

She blows out her breath when we get away from him and looks at me in bewilderment. "Wow." I can sense her agitation.

"Seems like you have an admirer," I mutter, none too happy.

Brittany brushes it off. "He's just been drinking." Then, her arm snakes around my waist. "But I am hoping he's not the only admirer I have," she says leaning into me.

I tenderly smile; she does that to me "You know the answer to that," I say as I kiss her.

"The gala was fun," Brittany says with relief as we walk through the parking garage. "I've never had fun at one before."

"It was fun, but I'm starving. What do you want to eat?" The food was a very thin spread of hors d'oeuvres.

"Wendy's!" she cheers.

"Wendy's it is," I say and point the truck toward the closest one.

I go to the drive through and pick us up some food, then continue home.

"Are you eating all the fries?" I accuse as I see Brittany sneak another fry out of the bag.

She turned wide, innocent eyes to me. "No, not at all."

I cock my head at her. "Mhmm," I hum doubtfully.

A few minutes and four fry sneaks later, I demand, "Okay, hand over the bag."

Brittany cries, "I'm sorry! You can't expect me to hold a bag of hot fries and not sneak some."

"I never will again, I promise. Hand it over," I insist.

"I promise, I'll stop. There are still plenty of fries," she claims pitifully as I take the bag from her.

I eye her as I pull into the driveway. "I hope so."

We proceed into Brittany's house, where much to my amusement, she hikes up her dress and sits cross legged on the floor of the living room. I remove my jacket, untuck my shirt, and untie my tie, letting it hang loose around my neck. Brittany had been unpacking the food but stops short when she sees me. My chest swells at her notice. I like that she so obviously finds me attractive.

"Matt?" she asks breathlessly.

"Yes?"

"Will you promise to only wear a tux if I'm with you?" she asks while eyeing me as I sit on the floor across from her.

I laugh ruefully. "Absolutely, baby, if you promise to only wear heels like that when I'm with you."

Brittany looks over at her shoes, now discarded, and cracks a wicked smile. "Deal."

We eat on the floor of the living room, laughing and talking as the evening continues. We end up watching a movie (not a Disney movie) snuggled on the couch. She falls asleep against me again, and I think it's cute that her and Grady both can't make it through a movie. I hold her throughout the show and reluctantly wake her when it's over. I like that she feels comfortable enough with me to sleep in my arms. She groans and goes deeper into my shoulder, and I can't help but love it when she does that.

"Time to go to sleep, sweet girl," I whisper.

She groans again but opens her eyes and lifts her head.

"You'll come swim with us tomorrow?" she asks sleepily.

"I'll be there," I confirm.

She smiles only half conscious and slowly raises up off me to walk me to the door. I have to say going home every night is getting old.

Chapter 17

Matt

Roughly a week after the nurses' gala, I am swinging with Brittany in my arms, trying to think of a way to bring up a particular topic without spooking her. She has a tendency to act like a little deer in headlights when I talk about progressing our relationship, and I don't want to do anything stupid. Although she was surprisingly calm when I told her I loved her, and she even told me she loved me too, I don't want to push my good luck. It took weeks of swinging on her porch every night before she finally agreed to go on a date with me. Fortunately for me, it wasn't too many weeks later when she admitted she loved me. I smile at the memory. Time to take the plunge.

"So," I clear my throat nervously, "I was thinking that maybe, if you wanted to, you and Grady could come to lunch with my folks after church on Sunday."

Brittany looks up at me with wide eyes and, to my utter shock, giggles. "I wondered when you were going to ask. Truthfully, I thought you didn't want me to meet your parents until Maddy said you were trying not to scare me off."

I laugh in relief. "True. Be warned, they can be enthusiastic." I look down at her face. "You want to meet them, really?" I ask uncertainly.

"Of course," she says with a smile. "I didn't want to bring it up, but you've spent a lot of time with my parents, and I've gotten to know Maddy really well."

I snort; that was true. She talks to Maddy more than I do. Every day, if my suspicions are correct.

"Oooh, do you think Maddy would come home to eat with us too?" she asks but doesn't wait for me to respond. She whips out her phone and calls Maddy right on the spot. I really don't mind; I love that she gets along with my sister. However, I start to get a little annoyed as their conversation goes on. They are now discussing clothing options.

I decide to try my hand at distracting her, reminding her that this is my time. Time for just the two of us. The phone is at her ear opposite to me, so I start kissing from her cheek and to her free ear.

"Um...Maddy, I have to go," Brittany says breathlessly before she hangs up without waiting for a response.

I claim her mouth in a way that should banish all thoughts of my sister or my family and am pleased when I hear a little whimper come from her. I pull back before getting carried away, proud of my effect on her.

"Wow," Brittany says with heavy-lidded eyes. "I'd say you made your point, but I wouldn't mind you making it again."

"I love that you love my sister, but there are boundaries. This is my time," I admonish.

"Remind me again, will you?" Brittany asks softly, and who am I to not do what the lady asks?

* * *

A week later, we are loading up my truck after church to head to my parents' house.

CHAPTER 17

"Cool! Mom, look! This booster has Spiderman on it!" Grady calls as I buckle him in the backseat of my truck.

"Yeah, Buddy," Brittany says in distraction as she climbs in up front. Despite her initial excitement, Brittany now seems nervous.

"You okay?" I ask as I settle into the driver's seat and take her hand.

She nods, but her smile doesn't reach her eyes. I don't move until she reluctantly speaks. "What if they don't like me, or Grady? What if they don't want you to take on all of this?"

"That's impossible. They'll love you and Grady, and they'll completely overwhelm you with their love and adoration," I say with certainty.

She smiles, but it still doesn't reach her eyes.

I start the truck and head toward my parents, me and Grady playing I Spy along the way. Brittany remains very still and quiet throughout the drive. When I pull into my parents' driveway, I feel the tension mounting on Brittany's side of the car.

"Um...Matt?" she says with concern.

"Whoa, Momma, are we at a museum?" Grady asks from the back with awe in his voice.

I wince. I maybe forgot to mention that my parents are incredibly wealthy.

"Sorry, I forgot to tell you," I say with genuine remorse.

She turns wide, panicked eyes to me and almost stutters over her words. "You forgot?"

I shrug helplessly. "I don't know, it's just my parents' house. I don't really think about it."

She keeps staring at me, and I feel totally sure that is not a good thing.

"Momma, do people live here?" Grady keeps going.

"Yeah, Buddy, my parents live here. This is where Maddy stays when she's in town," I explain lightly, hoping my nonchalant tone will resonate with Brittany. It does not.

I'm still a little unsure of Brittany's being unsure when we are both startled by her passenger door flying open.

"You didn't tell her?" Maddy asks me in outrage after taking in my and Brittany's expressions.

I shrug helplessly again. "I didn't think about it. You could've mentioned it too," I mutter.

Maddy rolls her eyes at me and addresses Brittany. "Take a deep breath." Brittany follows Maddy's lead, and I find myself taking notes. "It's fine. Our parents are super down-to-earth people; they just have a lot of money. They are going to adore you. Buck up, buttercup, it's show time."

"Buck up, buttercup!" Grady calls, giggling from the back.

I get out and move to the back to unbuckle Grady, picking him up and setting him on the ground. We walk around the truck, and Brittany takes Grady's hand and kneels in front of him. "Remember what we talked about, Buddy. When we are in someone else's home, we ask before we touch anything, right? Stay close to me, okay? And try not to yell. Use your inside voice."

Grady nods along seriously, picking up on Brittany's anxiety, and I feel terrible. I glance at Maddy for help but she's glaring at me.

"Yes, Momma," Grady says seriously.

Brittany kisses his cheek and smooths his hair nervously while she tells him, "You're a good boy, Grady. I love you."

"I love you too, Momma," he says with concern.

Geez, nobody's going to Vietnam or anything.

Maddy punches my arm and gestures to Brittany, and I take her other hand. I look into her eyes and say, "I love you."

"I love you too," she says numbly, eyes still betraying her fear.

We head to the front of the house, and I have to admit that the Georgian plantation house does look a little like a museum. We don't even get up the walkway before the front door opens and Mom comes rushing toward us. "Matthew! Finally! Come in, come in!"

"Hey, Mom, I would like for you to meet Brittany Masters and her son, Grady," I announce after I hug her, gesturing to Brittany proudly.

Brittany extends her hand. "It's lovely to meet you. Your home is extraordinary," she says tentatively.

"Why, thank you. I'm a hugger, I hope you don't mind. Call me Grace," Mom says ignoring Brittany's hand and pulling her into a tight hug. She then shifts her focus to Grady and says, "You are the cutest little boy I've ever seen. Can I have a hug from you too?"

Grady looks to Brittany for permission; when she nods he goes straight into my mother's arms.

"Not too tight, Mom," Maddy says with an eye roll.

Mom rises back to her feet and takes Brittany's arm, leading her toward the kitchen "Brittany, dear, I do hope you treat your parents better than my kids treat me. You know they say moms nag, but I think I have the only kids in the country that nag me more than I nag them," she says with a laugh.

Maddy snorts as we followed them to the kitchen. Grady now stands close to me as Mom has absconded with Brittany, so I take his hand and kept him close.

"Cal, honey, look who's here," Mom calls as Dad walks up. "This is my husband, Cal."

"Nice to meet you," Brittany says, enveloped in another tight hug from my Dad. She looks for Grady, her eyes softening when she finds him with me. "This is my son, Grady," she says holding out her hand to him. Grady walks forward shyly, and my Dad crouches down. "You are a fine-looking young man. How old are you, Grady?"

Grady looks silently to his mom and Brittany nods. "I'm seven," Grady says in a small voice.

It's a little disturbing to see them like this. The entire time I've known Grady he's been nothing but totally outgoing, running up to strangers to talk to them. I wonder if his mother's nervousness is affecting him that much.

"Now, I didn't know what you liked, so we made the basics. I hope that's okay. Matthew, honey, come get drinks, would you?" Mom instructs.

I leave Brittany under Maddy's supervision and proceed to the middle of my parents' colossal kitchen to put ice in glasses. I know Mom already has lemonade and sweet tea on the table, so I don't worry about filling them.

When I get to the table, I'm not overly excited that Mom sits me across from Brittany instead of beside her or Grady. We all take our seats, and my Mom takes a breath from talking Brittany's ear off. Dad leaps at the chance and says, "Let's say grace."

We pass fried chicken, mashed potatoes, mac and cheese, green beans, and corn around the table, and again I wish I was beside Grady to help Brittany. She is both successfully engaged in conversation with my parents and making hers and Grady's plates. I see Grady staring uncertainly at his chicken when I take matters into my own hands. I get up and move around the table without interrupting the conversation and sit down in the empty chair beside the boy.

"You need help with your chicken, Buddy?" I whisper.

"I can do the chicken," he whispers worriedly, "but I don't like green beans and corn, and Mom didn't give me any mac and cheese."

I look at the back of Brittany's head as she answers a question from my Dad and say, "Tell you what, you eat three bites of corn and green beans and I'll give you some mac and cheese."

Grady visibly brightens. "Okay!"

I grab the mac and cheese and dip him some, whispering, "I'm watching you. No cheating."

He giggles as I move back to my original seat. I start to eat, and I'm pleased that during my absence, Maddy has stepped up and looked out

CHAPTER 17

for Brittany. I jump into the conversation, and before long, Brittany is laughing and talking like normal. Grady has taken three bites of green beans and corn and is working his way through the mac and cheese. I relax, because life is good.

After lunch we go to the family room, and I frown in resignation, not at all surprised at the display in the middle of the floor.

"Whoa," Grady breathes reverently beside me.

"You can say that again, Buddy," I say, glaring at my Mom, who is unrepentant.

Brittany and Maddy come in next, and Brittany stops short in shock. "Wow."

"Mom..." I start in warning.

Mom shakes her head and jumps in before I can finish my sentence. "I don't want to hear it, Matthew. I wanted to make sure Grady would be comfortable here, so I picked up a few things for him to play with. There is nothing wrong with that," she says defensively.

I glance at my dad and he shrugs, helpless. "You know your mother."

Grady tugs at my pants leg and I lean down. "Yeah, Buddy?"

"Can I play with those?" he asks in a whisper.

I look at Brittany, Grady following my gaze. She shrugs, looking back at me baffled.

"Absolutely, Bud. What do you want to play with first?" It looks like the entire toy section of Target is in my parents' living room, so understandably, it takes Grady a minute of perusing before he chooses Legos.

"Good choice, my boy. Bring those over here," my dad instructs.

I walk Grady and the Legos box over to the coffee table near Dad and we tear into it while Brittany, Maddy, and Mom get settled on the couches and chairs. The afternoon speeds by until finally Maddy announces she needs to get on the road home.

"We should probably go too," I say to Brittany.

"Aw, Mom, do we have to?" Grady whines. I think my mom is going to have a conniption fit of happiness right in front of us.

"You just come back here whenever you want to, sweet boy? Okay?" Mom comforts placatingly, pulling him into a tight hug.

"Mom, not too tight," I caution because I'm genuinely concerned about Grady's air flow.

Mom glares at me and Brittany giggles. "Thank you so much for everything, Grace. It was a wonderful day." She not only goes for my mom willingly but actually pulls her into a hug.

"You are wonderful, my dear. Absolutely wonderful," Mom says with conviction, and I hope to God she isn't crying because that would be so embarrassing.

We finish our goodbyes, then I take Brittany and Grady out to my truck. When we head down the drive, I look over at her and say, "Well?"

Brittany grins. "You were right. They are great. It was fun." She starts laughing as she adds, "Oh my word, the toys! Matt! What in the world?"

I groan. "I told you, she gets excited."

"Mom, can we go there again?" Grady asks from the back.

"Sure, Buddy, we'll go there again," she assures, lacing her fingers with mine on the middle console.

Chapter 18

Brittany

"So how did it go?" Lily asks me as soon as I reach her chair.

"Really well. We had fun," I say as I hang her treatment bag.

"Tell me all about it," she demands excitedly.

I tell her all about our visit with Matt's parents, and Lily delights in hearing about all the toys.

"He forgot to tell you?" she laughs. "Rich people, they are all the same," she says teasingly.

I laugh but am distracted by the notes in her chart. Since there is a lull in the conversation, I bring up my main concern. "They changed your treatment, Lily," I say softly.

She sighs. "Noticed that, huh?"

I frown at her obviously. It's kind of my job.

"I guess the other treatments weren't doing much, so I agreed to bump it up one little notch. It's not even really helping with my energy like it should. If these don't do much, I'm going to stop," Lily confesses.

I stay quiet for as long as I can until I can't help myself. "I can't help but feel you are giving up, Lily."

She eyes me sadly. "I'm sorry you feel that way."

I stare at her, my emotions very close to the surface. I open my mouth to argue, but her look stops me cold. She doesn't look angry or even sad anymore. She looks determined.

"Please, Brittany, tell me more about your vacation next week." Her eyes are pleading, but I shake my head and look away.

I want her to fight. I want her to be strong. I don't want to lose her. I take a deep breath and remember Matt's words. Lily, in her own way, is being brave. She's choosing how to spend her remaining life. Who am I to judge her or take that away from her?

I swipe a tear from my cheek and say quietly, "Well, you know my parents have that house on the beach in Florida, so Derek and I are going to head down for the week."

"That sounds so fun. What do you usually do while you're there?" she asks, but her voice is tight.

I take another breath and share about the beach, letting her picture it all. We move on to talk about love, then life. We stop before we get to death.

That night when I write in my Lily journal, there are tear stains on the pages.

* * *

"How's Lily?" Matt asks because it's Thursday.

My eyes fill. "I don't know. Her treatments aren't working, and she's still refusing something stronger. It's not good, Matt. She may not have the whole year they thought she had originally."

He takes me into his arms and holds me as I cry.

"Tell me what's going on with you?" I ask after a while. Not that there's much I'm not aware of, I mean I saw him last night. I just want to hear him talk for a while, distract me from the inevitability of Lily's life.

CHAPTER 18

"Well, I think I'm gonna go by the school tomorrow and see if I can get my class list, stuff like that. Other than that, it's been a normal day. You're off tomorrow, right? Packing for the trip?"

My gut clenches because I don't want to go a whole week without seeing Matt. "Yeah. Grady has a playdate with Alison tomorrow. Her nanny is bringing her, and she happens to be Grady's kindergarten teacher, Denise, so that should be a fun reunion."

"So you won't see Gordon?" he asks a little too casually.

I give him a sly smile. "With any luck, no I won't."

He's happy about what I've said, then kisses me and sighs, "I'm gonna miss you two. A whole week, huh?"

"Yeah..." I say with just as much disappointment. "I wish you could come."

He is silent for a moment, but I can feel him thinking.

"Maybe next year," he says casually, but I can feel his growing tension as he waits for my response.

I glance at him curiously. "What do you mean?"

"I love you, Brittany. I love Grady. I would like for our relationship to continue progressing." He pauses, watching me closely. "Is that what you want?"

I look lovingly at the man sitting next to me who has treated me and my son with so much love and thoughtfulness. "Yes, that's what I want. So much," I whisper.

For the first time since we started dating, I don't feel fear. I don't feel afraid. Matt slowly chipped away at my concerns and doubts until I had no other choice but to trust him with my heart...and my son. I have no idea when it happened completely, but sitting here, right now, in this moment, I can say with certainty that I love him, and I want to marry him. There are a million questions about how that will work, but for tonight, in his arms, I choose to bask in the love and share honestly what is in my heart.

***

Matt

It's a beautiful day when you wake up and the sun is shining and the woman you love wants a future with you. A beautiful day, indeed.

It takes every ounce of my self-control to wait until supper time to see Grady and Brittany, especially given that they are leaving town tomorrow, but I know Brittany has a lot on her mind. I don't want to distract her from getting her stuff done before they leave.

I run over with pizza for dinner and walk into her house to find Grady playing on the living room floor and Brittany nowhere in sight.

"Dinner!" I call as I head to the kitchen.

Grady jumps up and runs to me, and I freakin' love it when he does that.

Brittany comes jogging from the bedrooms, grabs a piece of pizza, and shoves it into her mouth. "I have to keep packing," she says as she spins around and heads back up the hall in the space of a moment.

I get Grady settled at the kitchen table and take another piece of pizza back to Brittany. "You aren't done yet?" I ask, heading into Grady's room where she is packing his suitcase.

She huffs with overwhelming exasperation. "I got called in to work. Someone called in sick and I had to cover. I got home about an hour ago. I got nothing done today that I needed to. Look at the house! You don't even want to see the laundry room," she grumbles as she moves about, pausing quickly to grab the second slice of pizza from my hands.

"Why didn't you call me? I could have come over to help. What did you do with Grady?" I ask because I know her parents are out of town and still she didn't call me.

"You have your own stuff going on. I called Gordon to cancel the

CHAPTER 18

playdate, but he insisted that Denise pick Grady up and keep him. It was actually kind of a life saver, although it made me uncomfortable to have Grady go to someone's house that I've never been to," she acknowledges, zipping the suitcase. "I guess it worked out though."

I stand stock still and watch her set the luggage by the door before she walks to her room. My mind is racing and my temper flares. I try to get it under control, but before I get totally calm, Brittany comes back into the room and looks at me curiously. "What's wrong?"

"You left Grady with someone you don't know instead of calling me?" I ask, unable to hide my hurt and anger.

Brittany looks surprised. "I know Denise. She was his kindergarten teacher. I have never been to Gordon's house, which is where she kept the kids."

"But why didn't you call me, Brittany?" I ask in a slightly more demanding tone than I intend.

Brittany stares at me, and her soft words cut right to my heart. "I didn't think about it honestly, it all happened so fast. I just handled it."

I close my eyes and sit down in defeat on Grady's bed, rubbing a hand over my face. Maybe if I scrub hard enough the anger will dissipate.

"Matt, I don't understand why you're upset," Brittany says carefully.

I get up and face her, taking a deep breath before speaking. Unfortunately, my tone is not as measured as I want. "I can't believe you let Grady go off to that creep's house and you didn't even think about calling me. Didn't even consider it! I was free all day, Brittany. I could have helped! But you didn't even think about me."

Brittany stands there staring at me. "Grady is *my* son, Matt. I don't appreciate you acting like I left him in harm's way" she says in a very controlled but tight voice.

I roll my eyes. "I'm not saying you left him in harm's way, I'm just saying you allowed an uncomfortable situation instead of just calling me. I understand he is your son, but I love him too."

She just looks at me blankly. The fact that she still isn't seeing the issue makes me even angrier. "Is there even a scenario in your mind when you would think of calling me instead of some creep who just wants in your pants?"

Brittany steps back as if I slapped her, and I close my eyes in regret. "I'm sorry, I shouldn't have said that."

"Why would I call you when I already handled the issue?" she asks, angry herself.

"You don't have to handle everything yourself. That's the point! I don't want Gordon handling your issues. I want to handle your issues."

"The way I see it, I handled my own issue," Brittany says crossing her arms.

I gesture around. "You handled it yourself and look. You got no help and nothing done today, so how did that work out for you?" I spit. "Is this how you want things? Handle everything by yourself? I want to marry you, Brittany. I want to adopt Grady. I want to be a family. Is that what you want, or will Grady always be *your* son?"

Brittany glares at me and I glare back at her. This has maybe escalated to a place I did not intend for it to go, but I realize this a moment too late.

"Maybe you should go, Matt," Brittany says finally.

That hurts.

The pain and confusion must show on my face. She looks uncertain. Pissed, but uncertain. I hear her say, "I think we both need to cool down before we talk again."

I blow out a breath and nod, then silently walk away. I go to the kitchen and pull Grady into a hug.

"Have fun at the beach, Buddy. I'll miss you," I say, kissing his head.

"I'll miss you too, Matt," he answers before returning to his pizza.

I don't notice that Brittany has followed me into the kitchen. There is an odd look on her face as she watches me, but I don't ask, I just leave.

CHAPTER 18

Like she asked me to.

* * *

I spend the night being more aggressive than necessary when I put down my hardwood floor. I work until morning, and by the time I look outside, Brittany's car is gone. To Florida.

What crappy timing.

The next two days I work round the clock on the house. I can't sleep and I have too much energy. In light of this, my defenses are down Sunday evening and I accidentally answer my phone when Maddy calls.

"Why is Brittany avoiding my calls?" she demands.

I groan the answer. "We had a fight."

"What happened?"

I realize this can actually be a good thing. If I can convince Maddy that my perfectly constructed argument is sound (I've been working on for two days), she could maybe help with Brittany.

I explain the situation. "She didn't even call me, Mads. Didn't even think about calling me! How am I supposed to take care of her when she doesn't even call me? Clearly, she was uncomfortable with the situation, even I'm uncomfortable with Grady being at that creep's house, and yet she didn't call me. Then she said Grady is *her* son. Like I don't care about him too. Is that what it'll be like for the rest of our lives? Grady is *her* son? I want him to be my son too. She just won't let me in."

When I finish, there is a long silence, and I am proud of my perfectly logical and, more importantly, correct argument.

"You're a real idiot, you know that?" Maddy says dryly.

"What?"

"She gave birth to Grady. Has parented him for seven years. Alone. Who are you to step in and demand to be included? If she lets you in, fine.

But that's her decision. Maybe she should have thought about calling you, but you can't expect a single parent of seven years to suddenly know how to include a partner. She doesn't know how to do that, and you berating her into it is not going to help," my sister says fiercely.

I'm struck dumb, suddenly, completely realizing that I'm an idiot.

"I gotta go," I say quickly.

"Tell her to call me!" Maddy shouts before I hang up.

Chapter 19

Brittany

"What crawled up your butt?" Derek plops down on the couch next to me.

"Nothing," I say, trying to focus on my book, although I've read the same paragraph for the past hour and a half.

"You've been totally pissy since you got here. Trouble in paradise?"

I grunt, "Go away."

"Seriously, if I need to beat him up, just tell me. Cause I can totally take him," Derek says in a more serious tone.

I roll my eyes in exasperation; Derek is always looking for a fight.

I close my book because Derek is looking expectantly at me, and I'm obviously not going to get through this paragraph tonight.

"We had a fight." I explain the situation and who Gordon is and our previous experiences with him.

When I'm done, Derek snorts, "Hate to say this, B, but I'm with Matt."

My head whips back. "What?"

He continues, "Not that you put Grady in any harm or anything like that, but I get that Matt's trying to take care of you. You should let him. Besides, that Gordon guy does sound like a creep."

I shove my brother's shoulder. "First of all, you are supposed to be on my side, and secondly, I had the situation firmly under control. I'm not gonna let anyone tell me what to do or how to raise my son. He is being a little possessive."

Derek shakes his head, running on. "Nah, you're just being dramatic. I mean, he is being a *little* possessive. But as a guy, if I was trying to take care of my girl and she didn't even think about calling me when she needed help, I would be hurt."

I stare at him considering this. "Really?"

"Yeah. I mean, we all know you are capable, B. It's just that he wants to know you can rely on him too. That you'll turn to him when you need him."

"Of course, I would," I say defensively.

"Would you?" he argues.

"Why wouldn't I?" I challenge.

Derek eyes me pointedly. "I don't know. You had to work an extra shift and left Grady with some creepy guy's nanny, even if it is Grady's former teacher. Seems like the more logical thing to me would have been to call Matt and drop Grady with him."

Did I tumble down a rabbit hole and everything is opposite of what it should be? He's got me seriously thinking, which is surprising since I make it a point to not think too seriously about anything Derek has to say. He may just have a point here, though, and if Derek has a point and I was wrong it is most definitely opposite day.

"Think about it like this. He says he wants to marry you, right? Wants to adopt Grady. He's looking to know there is a place for him with you. That you'll make space for him. He is laying it all on the line and wants to know that, at some point, you'll trust him with the big stuff," Derek explains.

"I do trust him, though. That's the issue. I feel like it was all just blown out of proportion," I say with frustration.

"Was it really? I mean, he's gone pretty slow. It was a pretty big deal

CHAPTER 19

for you to leave Grady with him that one time, right? Then you tell him that in a pinch you left Grady with this weird guy's nanny? Again, as a guy, I would think that's symptomatic of a bigger issue. Like maybe you don't trust me."

I can tell Derek is sincere. He is starting to make sense, and that's disconcerting.

"Brittany, it's up to you, but you know, he's a pretty decent guy."

With that, he announces he's going for a run, and I'm alone once more on the couch. Maybe he's right. I mean, I stopped fighting. I fell pretty hard for Matt in fact. I gave him my heart, but maybe without realizing it, I have been holding back on his having more of a relationship with Grady.

* * *

Matt

I call Brittany immediately, but to my disappointment, Grady answers.

"Hey, Matt! You'll never guess...." With that, Grady spends the next twenty-five minutes telling me every single thing I've missed since he left the house yesterday morning. Normally, I would have enjoyed listening to the little guy, but I am a little anxious right now.

"I'm glad you are having fun, Buddy."

"I wish you were here too," he says finally.

"Me too, Grady. Can I talk to your Mom?"

I pull my ear away from the phone as Grady yells for his mom without moving the phone away from his mouth. I wait somewhat impatiently for Brittany to come to the phone, but when I hear her murmur to Grady, my breath catches.

"Hey," she says softly.

"Hey," I reply.

I pause, gathering my courage. "I'm sorry, Brittany. I was a jerk. We can figure this out, right? I love you, and I just want to be there for you and for Grady."

I wait for her to respond. I hear her sigh in relief and say, "I love you, Matt. We'll figure it out. I'll try to rely on you and include you more. It's just going to be a...process."

"I'm good with a process, baby. I just want to be in it with you. That's all I want," I insist.

"Thank you, Matt, that means a lot to me."

I ask in relief, "Forgive me?"

"Of course."

I think I can hear her smile. "I miss you. We still have the whole week to go," I groan.

Brittany snorts and says ironically, "I know. For the first time ever, I think I would rather be home than at the beach."

"Grady gave me a rundown of what y'all have been up to. Are you having fun at least?"

"He's been begging to call you...I wasn't sure..." she says uncertainly.

"I always want to hear from Grady, Brittany, always. I always want to hear from you too," I insist. "I guess I just needed a sledgehammer to help me hear you," I admit with a wry chuckle.

Now she outright laughs. "Am I correct in assuming that sledgehammer's name is Maddy?"

"You are correct. I had a perfectly logical argument I'd been working on. Then I laid it all out for her and she calls me an idiot." I laugh with Brittany. "She was right, though. I'm glad she helped me understand. I guess I didn't see it from your point of view."

Brittany responds with new determination in her voice. "I love you

CHAPTER 19

Matt. I just need to work on letting you into my life a little more."

"Like I said, baby, I just want to be there for you and Grady. Always. I love you," I state reassuringly. I want to make my feelings absolutely clear so there is no confusion.

"I love you too," she says sweetly.

"And before I forget, Maddy wants you to call her." I then mention off handedly, but with plenty of curiosity, "What's going on with her and Derek anyway?"

She lowers her voice, continuing, "I don't know, but she won't talk about it, and he is a huge grump."

I frown in concern not liking the sound of this at all. "I hope she moves home. She's been looking at jobs in the area."

"Me too. I would love for her to be close."

We fall silent for a minute, listening to each other breathe. "I miss you, Brittany."

"I miss you too," she says with a trace of longing. "I should probably get Grady to bed now, though."

"Love you. Talk to you tomorrow."

We hang up and I have never in my life been so tempted to drive to Florida just to hug someone.

* * *

Brittany

"Finally!" Maddy exclaims when I call her after Grady goes to bed. "Just because you and my idiot brother have a fight doesn't mean jack to us. I'm a little offended you thought you had to avoid me because of a fight with my brother."

I take a breath to plunge in but she keeps going.

"I mean, I had a serious issue to discuss with you. Serious. And you wouldn't pick up the phone. What in the world!?" she admonishes dramatically.

"Point made. I'm very sorry, Maddy." I'm enjoying the salty sea breeze from the deck of my parents' beach place with Derek, who is sitting on the other side reading a book. I pretend not to notice that his head twitched when I said her name.

"Forgiven. I had the most awful date I need to tell you about," she says with exasperation.

"A date?" I ask in surprise.

Derek's head jerks up, and he stares at me for a moment before storming off the porch.

Well, that could've gone better.

"You wouldn't believe this guy, Brittany. Tried to sell me insurance. Insurance! He was a wine taster too," she says disgusted.

"Ugh, did he slurp, breathe, and gargle the wine?" I ask with equal disgust, but mine is mixed with amusement.

"Yes! It was so embarrassing!"

"Sorry you had a crappy date," I say sincerely.

"It's fine. Another one bites the dust. The search continues," she sighs in desolation.

I hesitate before asking, "Maddy, what happened with Derek?"

Maddy is so silent I can almost hear her shoulders slump. "Nothing happened. He asked for my number that day at your house when he walked me to my car, but he's never called. It's surprising and a little hurtful since I thought we were both feeling it, but whatever. As I said, the search continues."

Hmm. Interesting. I'm not sure what in the world Derek is thinking, not that we regularly talk about his dating life. I guess he could have a girlfriend I don't know about.

CHAPTER 19

"Are you still thinking of moving home?"

"Yeah. Actually, I've had a couple call backs from a few firms. Maybe by the end of the year I'll be home. I don't know."

"That's great! Keep me updated. Grady and I would love it if you were home," I say wistfully.

"Me too. Never had a nephew before. It's gonna be fun."

We chat a few more minutes before I eventually hung up, picking up my book and reading with the waves crashing as my soundtrack.

"Did you say she was moving home?" Derek asks from the door.

"Eavesdropping, detective?" I ask coolly, not lowering my book.

He simply grunts. "It's a small house. Sound carries."

I continue as if I don't care. "What's it to you?"

He is silent for so long I actually wonder if he went inside again. Then he sits down in the chair he was in earlier and grunts, "I don't know." He sounds miserable.

I lower my book and look at him. "Why don't you just call her and ask her?" I suggest obviously.

He looks out toward the ocean for a long moment, then gets up and walks back inside.

Chapter 20

Brittany

When Saturday comes, I do something I never ever do. I get up at five in the morning to put Grady in the car and head home. I almost always wait until the last possible moment, wanting to soak in as much beach time as possible, but it has been the longest week of my life without seeing Matt. Especially with our fight right before Grady and I left. First it was because I was anxious to resolve our conflict, then because it was resolved, and now I just wanted to be near him. I frankly can't take it anymore, so I got the car loaded, kissed my parents over their coffee, and put a sleeping Grady in the car.

Five hours later, we are pulling into the driveway, and to my delight, Matt comes rushing out of his house.

"Momma! It's Matt!"

"I see!" I throw the car in park and hop out, rushing into my man's arms.

"I missed you so much. I love you. I missed you." Matt breaths against my hair.

"I missed you too. Longest week of my life," I say earnestly.

He pulls back from our embrace and goes straight to the back of the car, unbuckling Grady and lifting him in his arms.

CHAPTER 20

"Missed you, Buddy. Did you have a good time?"

Grady nods emphatically. "Pop and I went fishing. I wish you were there, though. Can you come next time?"

Matt glances at me hopefully but only says, "We'll see. Come on, let's help your mom get your bags in."

I turn the car off and open the garage door, having been too distracted to do this before. We grab the stuff from the back, and I follow Grady and Matt into the house. I dread going in. I left the house a mess, and I will be buried under laundry for the rest of the weekend.

I stop short entering the kitchen. It is sparkling. The floors are cleaned and steamed, the counters are cleared and wiped down. I look around the living room and it is picked up and cleaned too. Everything is neat and tidy, and if I'm not mistaken, the carpet's shampooed? The distinct smell of disinfectant is in the air, and just when I think it can't get better, I take my bag straight to the laundry room and drop it, gasping in shock.

Laundry. Piles of it, neatly cleaned and folded, sorted by Grady's and mine in separate baskets.

Matt comes up behind me to ask, "You okay?"

I turn with tears in my eyes. "Did you clean my house and do my laundry?"

He looks a little sheepish. "Didn't have much to do with you and Grady gone, so I thought I'd help."

I stare at him as a million wonderful thoughts flood my head, like how I thought I could ever not love him, invite him into our lives, and spend forever with him.

"Thank you," I say softly, overwhelmed, as I try like the dickens to hold back tears. "No one has ever done anything like this for me."

"I love you. I'll do anything I can for you, Brittany," Matt says sincerely.

I reach up and kiss him in what was meant to be a soft and chaste kiss, but then the smell of Pine-Sol hits me and the fact that he cleaned my bathrooms makes me want to jump him in a not-so-Christian, ladylike fashion. I may have gotten a little carried away, so I jerk back when I hear Grady's voice.

"Mom? Are you guys kissing?" he asks from below us.

I look down at him trying to focus, my thoughts a little jumbled from the smell of cleaning supplies coupled with Matt's kiss.

"Yeah, Buddy, we are."

"Alison says only mommies and daddies kiss. Matt, are you going to be my daddy?"

I close my eyes and remind myself that only terrible people have thoughts about hurting children. Dang that Alison! I crouch down and say, "Maybe, Buddy, but we are just keeping Matt as a good friend until then, okay?"

"Okay," my son says with disappointment, then walks back to his room.

"Well, that cut me right to the heart," Matt says miserably.

Yeah, me too.

"Sorry. I keep trying to manage his expectations, but he really wants you to be his daddy." I take one of his hands.

"What do you mean, manage his expectations?" he asks me.

"He's asked before and I told him I didn't know. I explained that you were a friend for now. It's all he can really understand at this point."

Matt looks tortured. "I don't want to be just a friend."

I'm not really sure what he is saying, but I nod. "I don't really want that either. I don't really kiss my friends like that," I add trying to lighten the mood.

He is watching me very carefully. "Want me to order dinner? I thought I would go pick something up. I can take Grady with me while you get settled here if you want."

"Chinese?" I ask hungrily.

CHAPTER 20

He kisses my nose affectionately. "Sure, baby."

"Grady, come put your clothes away!" I call as I take his basket to his room.

A few minutes later, he comes skidding into the laundry room to pick up his clothes and I help him back to his room to put everything away. By the time we are done, Matt has called in the order. He takes Grady's hand to head to his truck to pick up the food.

I try not to laugh when I hear Matt explaining, "This is what men do, Grady. We hunt and provide for the family."

"I thought we were picking up Chinese food?" Grady asks in confusion.

"There are many ways to hunt in this day and age," he says as the cab door closes.

I call Lily while I'm starting laundry. I missed seeing her at her appointment this week and want to check in on her.

"How was the beach?" she greets upon answering.

"Amazing. I missed Matt, though," I say honestly.

Lily giggles ruefully. "Oh how the mighty have fallen. That's great."

"I really do. You won't believe this...but he actually cleaned my house and did my laundry while I was gone. This in addition to the fact that he already does my yard work," I brag. I can't help it. I feel like I have literally captured a unicorn.

Lily huffs, "Wow. I had no idea a man was capable of that. I can't get Joe to find the laundry basket with his clean underwear, much less clean an entire house, do the laundry, and finish the yard work."

I laugh with bubbly humor. "I know, right. I'm positively floating. But how are you? How did your treatment go?"

"I'm good. I have a summer cold right now, but other than that I'm fine. Treatment was good. Some of your other nurses came over to chat with me since you were away. It was actually kind of fun."

"Really?" I ask in surprise.

"Yeah, it was nice." She heaves a heavy breath. "I gotta go. Joe is coming, and I'm supposed to be resting," she says miserably. "Thanks for calling, Brittany. I'll see you Thursday."

I chuckle at Joe's militant care concern of Lily. Poor guy might work himself into an early grave right next to Lily if he isn't careful.

I've got the laundry running and have put everything else away just in time for Grady and Matt to come back with the food.

"We hunted, Momma!" Grady proclaims proudly.

"I see that!" I say with a happy smile to Matt, who winks.

"Matt, can you come to my open house and meet my new teacher with me?" Grady asks suddenly as we sit down to eat.

"Sure, Buddy, when is it?"

I tell him the date and he smiles in relief after consulting the calendar on his phone. "My open house is the next night, so I'll be there at yours, Grady."

We eat together while filling Matt in on Grady's favorite parts of vacation. Then Matt and Grady play on the floor in the living room while I finish the laundry and unpack our suitcases. I give Grady a bath and put him to bed, coming back into the living room to find Grady's toys neatly put away and Matt waiting for me on the couch. He reaches for me with welcoming arms, and I snuggle into his side. *Geez, I missed this.*

"Me too," he murmurs against my hair.

I really should have more self-awareness when I'm with him. I can't recall if I've said something out loud or if it's just in my head.

"Brittany, can we talk about the future?" Matt asks apprehensively.

I sit up straighter in his arms so I can look at him. For the first time, I am certain of what I want in the future, however, I see obstacles in our way. If our argument before the trip has taught me anything, it's that

CHAPTER 20

we both have a lot to learn to make this relationship work.

"Where do you see us going, Brittany?" he continues hesitantly.

I think back to our fight, when he said he wanted to marry me and adopt Grady, and I wonder now if he's having second thoughts. I swallow and take a deep breath. "I want to be a family," I admit for the first time out loud. He looks relieved, but doesn't say anything. "Don't you want that too?" I ask hesitantly.

"Of course, I do, I've said as much. It's just...well, you've never said. I want to be on the same page. I want to adopt Grady. I want to be his dad," he shares earnestly.

His confession causes my heart to clench and makes it hard for me to breathe. "I want that too."

He looks relieved again, but I can tell there is still something on his mind. "I was thinking...for the school year, maybe I could pick Grady up from after care when I'm done teaching? My time varies a bit, but it'll still probably be before your shift ends."

I consider this carefully and, although it's uncomfortable for me, I say "If that's what you want to do. I would appreciate it, and I'm sure Grady would love it." This is the first step I take in letting Matt into our lives. If he wants to help and spend more time with Grady, I need to let go of control and let him. Side note—how lucky am I that this man is making such an effort for me and my son?

Matt smiles brilliantly at me. The words have cost me and, if he noticed, he doesn't mention it. His smile is appreciation enough I suppose. "I would like you to let me know when you get him though, and when y'all are home. I do have a thing about knowing where my son is," I say pointedly.

"Of course, I wouldn't dream of it any other way," Matt laughs.

"Thanks for agreeing to come to his open house. He really wants you to meet his new teacher and see his school."

"I can't wait," he says sweetly.

The only thing I'm unclear of after our brief chat about the future, and the following make-out session, is exactly where we stand. I mean, we both want to be a family, so…are we engaged now? I keep these questions to myself, but this doesn't help me fall asleep that night.

Chapter 21

Brittany

A few weeks later, after a particularly brutal double shift, I drive home with the radio blaring to stay awake. It is seven in the morning and, although the sun is shining brightly, my mind and body beg for the release of sleep. I walk into the house to find Matt making Grady breakfast, evidence of the new normal.

"Good morning," Matt greets me with a kiss.

"Momma!" Grady runs to me and gives me a huge hug.

"My two favorite guys! I missed you," I say giving him a tight hug back.

"Hungry?" Matt asks, offering oatmeal.

I really don't want to eat, I want to sleep, but my stomach growls, and I want to stay up until they leave.

"Sure, thank you. So, what did you guys do last night?" I ask, making conversation to stay awake.

Grady and Matt exchange a glance that I immediately file in my mind to think about later.

"We finished Grady's homework, we played around a bit, then I tucked him into bed. Normal evening," Matt says casually, setting a bowl of oatmeal in front of me.

"Thanks. Normal evening, huh?" I ask suspiciously.

"Momma, look at my quiz from yesterday! I got a check mark!" Grady waves the paper in my face proudly.

"That's great, Buddy. I'm proud of you," I say, giving his head a kiss.

"Grady, go get your book bag, we gotta go," Matt says tapping his watch.

Matt comes around the bar and kisses my temple as I shovel oatmeal into my mouth. "Tonight? You're off, right?"

I nod. "Yep, tonight. Do you want to pick Grady up today?" I ask. "Or I can tell him to ride the bus since I'm home."

He shakes his head no. "Don't worry about it. I'll get him. Sleep a little later." He kisses me in earnest, then I lean forward to hug and kiss Grady, wishing him a good day. The second the door closes, I pull my scrubs shirt over my head and head back to my bedroom, finally allowing myself to collapse in the bed.

* * *

I wake up a blessed eight hours later feeling like a new person. I shower and dress in a light sundress since Matt is taking me out tonight. I decide to let my hair air dry and proceeded to the kitchen for a Diet Coke.

On my way, I fold up the blanket on the couch where Matt made his bed the previous evening. A new routine began with the start of the school year. I take Grady to school every day, Matt picks him up, and we eat dinner together almost every night.

I am almost always on day shift now, given recent scheduling changes at the hospital and clinic, but as a manager I have to cover shifts that no one else can. As such, I have the occasional night or double shift. In these instances, despite my protests, Matt insists on sleeping on the couch so Grady can sleep in his own bed.

I have to admit, coming home to the two of them makes my heart feel whole in a way I never thought possible. Although it hasn't been without its bumps, allowing anyone else into my son's world to take care of him and discipline him and love him was difficult at first. In fact, it's still difficult. It feels wrong a bit, like I am outsourcing my job. The adoring looks Grady only gave me are shared now with Matt. The questions he used to ask me are also asked to Matt. Grady doesn't only want to hang out with me anymore, he wants to hang out with Matt. I struggled silently for the first couple of weeks as I worked to tamp down my fears and jealousy.

The transition became easier one Saturday at my parents' pool. My parents, Matt, and I were on the deck munching on fruit and watching Grady splash around. He was working on his different jumps and dives until he decided to take a break for a snack. Afterwards, he was following Dad out to the shed in the back corner of the yard when he slipped and fell in the deep end of the pool without his floaties on. Before I even had a chance to get up from my chair, Matt was up and diving into the pool, then hauling Grady back up the steps. Other than spluttering a little bit, Grady was fine. He is actually a pretty strong swimmer and doesn't really need the floaties anymore, but I'm just not ready to let him loose without them.

Once we all took turns determining Grady was fine, much to his annoyance, we all returned to the deck. Matt didn't join us; he decided to stay in the pool with Grady. I went to join them and found Matt hovering over Grady with concerned attention. When I asked him if he was okay, Matt turned to me with the color still drained from his face and said, "We could have lost him. Just like that." He shook his head, as if to clear the terrible thoughts from his mind, and said, "I'm fine, I just need to be near him a little longer."

I'll never forget the look of sheer terror on his face as he thought through that. I realized then that it wasn't just about me anymore, or about Grady's attention and affection. Matt is a goner too. He loves Grady with a fierceness similar to my own, and for that I can freely share. I can share Grady's affection with the man who loves us with selfless devotion. It's the least I can do.

I look at the clock and get a move on; the guys will be home any minute. It's Friday and officially date night. With my parents back from the beach house, they've agreed to keep Grady overnight so we won't have to get back early.

I am elbow deep in makeup, with Maddy on video chat chatting as I get ready, when I hear the door open.

"We're home!" Matt calls.

"Back here!" I yell through the bedroom. Soon, both my guys invade my room and hunt me down in the bathroom as I apply one last swipe of mascara.

"Hi, Momma." Grady hugs my middle.

"Hey, baby." Matt kisses my lips above Grady's head.

"Hey guys, say hi to Aunt Maddy!" I point to my phone propped on the counter.

They greet her in unison, and we all catch up as I finish my hair.

"Tell me about your day," I ask Grady and he immediately launches in, including sharing every word Alison said throughout the day.

Yes, she's in his class again. No, I still can't control my eye rolls.

When he finishes, I tell him to go pack a bag for Gran and Pop's house and walk to my closet for some shoes. I put them on as Matt watches me appreciatively.

"How is Lily?" he asks.

I sigh, my heart heavy. "Not well. She is going downhill much more quickly than expected. I sat with her for over three hours yesterday. Joe is a total mess. The treatments aren't helping and she's refusing to take them anymore. It won't be long until she has to tell her family."

CHAPTER 21

Matt frowns in commiseration. "I'm sorry, I know this is difficult for you."

"I wish there was more I could do, there's just...nothing. I mean, her system is shutting down. It's a slow and painful process. I just hope she can make it through the holidays."

Matt squeezes my shoulder, assuring me. "You are doing everything you can just by being there with her."

I know this, but his support feels so nice. I return to touching up my makeup a little in the bathroom mirror as Matt watches. "I hope you aren't disappointed now that you've seen behind the curtain," I say self-consciously under his gaze.

He laughs. "On the contrary, I'm fascinated. It's like watching Wonder Woman put on her utility belt."

I kiss him before I help Grady with his bag, negotiating how many action figures he can take to Gran and Pop's house.

* * *

Tonight's date is dinner and a movie, with some ice cream after the show. It' the perfect evening, just me and Matt for the whole night. I wish it doesn't have to end. Matt drives us home, and I spot something odd on my front porch. He pulls into my driveway and comes around, opening the door for me as I look closer, wondering what it is. The porch is covered in citronella candles, just like the ones Matt first gave me months ago. Handmade hearts cut from construction paper hang from the ceiling covering the porch. Matt takes my hand and leads me up the steps, walking me through the hearts. He sits me on the swing and kneels in front of me.

"The first time I saw you, you were greeting Grady off the bus and I thought there had never been a more beautiful woman with more love for her child. I thought I was destined to live beside a happy family, admiring you from a distance. Then I met Grady, so rambunctious and full of energy, telling me how his mommy needed a husband." He pauses and chuckles at the memory. "I have to admit, I was taken with him, and with you. When I heard the chains of this swing creek that first night, I couldn't have kept myself away from you even if I tried."

I officially start crying. Not the cute kind.

"I spent weeks on this porch, swinging with you and falling more and more in love with you and your son. I cherish those memories and want a lifetime to make a million more just like them, right here, on this porch swing. Brittany Masters, I love you. I love Grady like he was my own. I want to love and adore you both for the rest of my life. Will you marry me and make us a family?"

"Yes" comes out as a choked, sobbing mess, but Matt pulls me into his arms and kisses me anyway. After, he pulls back and captures my hand, slipping a ring on my finger.

"Grady helped me pick out the ring. He said the two smaller diamonds could represent me and him, with the bigger diamond in the middle being you because you are so pretty." He smiles and kisses me lightly. "I prefer to think of it as two people making one big family."

I'm crying again and clinging to him as if my tears are going to drown me. My fiancé—fiancé!—holds me close, whispering how much he loves me into my ear and kissing my face softly. Eventually, after I calm down, he backs us up to the swing and pulls me onto his lap. I cuddle into his chest and we sway, listening to the chains creek and watching the candles flicker.

"This is beautiful, Matt. Thank you. I can't begin to describe how happy you make me," I say emotionally.

"Grady helped me make the hearts. We each wrote something we love about you on each one," Matt says sweetly.

"Really? Oh!" I get up excitedly and start collecting them.

CHAPTER 21

Makes me peanut butter and jelly sandwiches, your strength and determination is written on the first one. "Gee, I wonder which one came from who," I giggle.

Matt smiles. "He came up with each one by himself. I didn't even help him. I was very proud of that and so was he."

I take down each heart, tearing up again as I read each one. "This is too much, Matt. You are too good to me," I say when I'm done, a stack of hearts in my hand detailing a person I'm not completely sure I am.

"You deserve all this and more, Brittany. I'm gonna spend a lifetime proving it to you."

We sit on the swing, me cuddled into his side like so many of the nights we've spent before.

"What kind of wedding do you want?" I ask Matt.

"A quick one," he says with a mischievous grin. "What about you?"

"I don't know, I've never really thought about it. I hate for it to be too much, though." I wonder suddenly who pays for a single mom's wedding, my parents or do I?

"We'll pay for the wedding," Matt says, reading my thoughts.

I consider my savings account. "Courthouse it is!" I say teasingly.

Matt chuckles and soothes me. "I have some money set aside."

"I don't want you to spend all your money on a wedding. Surely something simple will be fine. Maybe at your parents' house?" I muse out loud.

"Careful, baby," Matt laughs. "Don't open Pandora's box unless you really mean it."

"Well, I wouldn't want anything huge and fancy. But something for fifty people outside at your parents' house might be nice." I warm to this idea the more I think of it. His parents' property is beautiful and would be the perfect place for a small event.

"Mom would love that, but you know it'll be hard to keep her focused. She'll take over and before you know it, the event will be completely different than what you originally wanted," he warns.

"You know, I don't really have an opinion on it, except I do want it to be rather small. Everything else is just fluff," I say simply.

"You should talk to Maddy before we talk to Mom. I'm not sure if this is a good idea or not," he says honestly.

"I just don't want you spending all your money on a wedding. Something small at your parents' house couldn't be that expensive, surely." Although, with his mother coordinating, anything is possible.

"Don't worry about money, baby. I have a trust fund," Matt says quietly.

I lean back to look at him. "What?"

He tries to play it off, returning, "Not a huge one, but it's a nice little nest egg. Besides if we have it at my parents' house, they will insist on paying." He then grunts, "They'll probably insist on paying anyway."

"I don't know how I feel about that," I say honestly.

"It's not really a big deal. They are generous people." I'm opening my mouth to protest, but he keeps talking, changing the subject. "So... to the more important question, when are you thinking?" he asks probingly.

I consider this and share my dream. "You know, I would love to be married before the holidays. To spend the holidays as a family, Grady would love that."

"I would love that too," Matt says with another sweet kiss on the temple.

"Do you think it's possible? It's the last week in September as it is. That's only what, a month and a half, two months maybe?" I ask in concern.

Matt puzzles it over before saying, "If you want my mom to do it, she'll do it. Gladly. Gleefully. Would your Mom have an issue with that?"

Hm, would she? "I don't know. I could ask her."

CHAPTER 21

I become lost in thought, and I remember something that I'm hesitant to bring up. "Speaking of your parents..." I start.

"Yes?" Matt prompts with a grimace.

"Christmas," I state.

"Ah," Matt breathes with understanding.

"I think we need to talk to them. They have to have a limit. We can't let them shower Grady with so much stuff. It's not healthy. He'll be spoiled rotten, and then nothing will be special," I explain hurriedly in concern.

"I completely agree. We should sit down and talk to them about that soon though, because there is a good chance Mom has already started shopping," he says wincing.

Now I am worried about how that will go over. I'm pulled from my concerns when Matt says, "We should call your parents. Grady knows I was planning to ask you tonight."

"He does?" I ask in surprise. That's odd because Grady hasn't really gotten the hang of the whole secret thing yet.

"He does. I asked his permission, and then I had him help me with the hearts."

"That is so sweet," I say as I take out my phone and video chat my mom.

"Well?" she asks excitedly. So, Grady couldn't keep a secret; he could just hold it in for a little while...good to know.

"We are getting married!" I squeal and show my ring to the camera.

"My goodness that's a gorgeous ring! I can't wait to see it in person tomorrow!" Mom says and shouts for Dad.

We repeat the news for him, and he congratulates us.

"Mom, Dad, we are thinking soon. We want to spend the holidays as a family. Would you have a problem with us possibly using Matt's parents' house?" I ask. We will pay for the wedding ourselves, of course."

"Whatever you kids want is fine with us," Mom and Dad laugh.

"Spending the holidays as a family is a sweet idea, Brittany. I'm so happy for you. Thank you, Matt, for taking care of our girl!" Mom is teary eyed, and Dad grunts in agreement in the background.

We hang up and call Maddy, who is adorably asleep when she answers. "H'lo?"

"Maddy wake up, we are getting married!" I yell.

I hear a bump and a thump. "Oof, what?!" Instantly aware, Maddy squeals, "Finally! Can I help plan the wedding? Can it be at Mom and Dad's? Can I be a bridesmaid?"

I giggle at her questions, and Matt dryly asks, "Maddy, did you just fall out of the bed?"

"Maybe...I had a rough week. I went to bed early," she justifies.

"We are thinking about Mom and Dad's, actually. You think Mom can handle it?" Matt questions.

Maddy laughs. "Matty, honey, she started planning it the day I sent the picture of you and Grady fishing."

"That doesn't really answer the question, though." Matt sighs, "In fact, it kind of gives me more reservations."

Maddy laughs again. "I say give her and Dad very clear parameters to work within. You know how she is. Lay out the boundaries clearly and she shouldn't have that big of an issue. Just make sure you give her boundaries with the expectation that she will go over, at least a little."

"Good idea, Mads."

"Congrats you two! I love you!" she cries.

"Love you too!" we say in unison, hanging up.

We sway quietly for another moment before Matt says, "Well, what do you think?"

"I think I want to spend the entire weekend with you and Grady because I've missed you. I think we should go see your parents tomorrow, and I think we should both go to bed so we can pick Grady up and take him and my parents to breakfast tomorrow morning," I

CHAPTER 21

say decidedly.

"Sounds like a plan. You should also invite Derek to breakfast," he suggests.

"Ooh, great idea," I agree, texting my brother immediately. Then a thought occurs to me. "I wonder if Maddy and Derek will be okay through the wedding."

"Why wouldn't they be?"

"Matt, Derek asked for Maddy's number and never called her. She tried to gloss over it, but it sounded like she was a little hurt. And Derek acted weird when I brought her name up at the beach. I don't know what's going on with him."

"They'll figure it out." He stands and tugs me up. "Get to bed, sweet girl. Tomorrow, we plan a wedding," he says with a kiss to end all kisses.

Chapter 22

Matt

The next morning, I meet Brittany outside, and can't deny the pride that fills my chest at her wearing my ring. We pick her parents and Grady up, and met Derek at a local breakfast place.

"Congrats, that's awesome," Derek says shaking my hand and hugging his sister.

We sit down and have breakfast, talking about future plans and wedding possibilities. Brittany and her mom put their heads together and talk about the event details, and I am thankful to be on the guys' end of the table. This conversation is about fishing conditions.

"Matt?" Grady asks as he studiously colors a paper menu.

"Yeah, Buddy?"

"Are you going to be my daddy now?" he asks very seriously.

"Yeah, Buddy, I am." I can finally say it. I've wanted so bad to say that.

"I'm glad," Grady says with a smile of relief.

"I love you, Grady," I say, pulling him into a hug.

"Love you too, Daddy."

Just like that, my heart explodes, and I hope to God the other guys don't see me tear up. When I glance up, I realize I don't have anything

CHAPTER 22

to worry about because they heard it and they teared up too.

* * *

"Oh, my gracious! Is that a RING?" Mom shrieks immediately as we enter the house.

Brittany laughs nervously, and Grady hides behind me. Smart move, kid. Mom takes Brittany's hand and inspects it closely. "Cal! Cal! Come in here! They are getting married!" Mom screams through the house. Never did need an intercom system even though the house is huge. "How pretty. Oh, honey, I'm so happy for you," Mom says, enveloping Brittany in a hug, then screaming over her shoulder more forcefully, "CAL!"

I pull my Mom off Brittany and sacrifice myself. "Mom, stop screaming. Please," I plead, hugging her.

"Sorry," she says, cheeks pinking. "I'm just so excited."

"Hey, kids," Dad says calmly as he leisurely walks down the stairs.

"Cal! They are getting married. Look!" Mom holds Brittany's hand up and excitedly waves it in the air.

Dad beams wider than I've seen before. "Congratulations! How wonderful!"

He hugs Brittany and then me, moving next to Grady.

"Come on," he says to Grady. "Just got a new box of Legos I think you'll like." He takes Grady's hand and pulls him into the living room.

I chuckle and stay with Brittany, who is watching me closely. I guess I should start. Mom is frantically asking questions and making plans, and I hold up my hands. "Mom. Calm down. Let's go sit down with Dad and Grady. We want to talk to you." Mom quiets her chatter but doesn't stop completely.

"Mom?" I ask once she and Dad are seated on the couch and Grady is playing Legos on the coffee table. Brittany and I sit down on the love seat across from them. I take a deep breath after Mom finally calms down. *God be with me.*

"Grace," Brittany starts, taking my hand in hers, "Cal, we would like to talk to you about the wedding."

"We want to have the wedding early-mid November so we can spend the holidays as a family," I say slowly, watching my Mom's eyes bug. Dad subtly takes her hand in his and I can tell she is biting her tongue to stay quiet.

"We really want a small, simple wedding that we can pay for ourselves," Brittany states, and I can tell it's my Dad's turn to bite his tongue.

"Maybe around fifty guests. I know it'll take some work to keep it that low, but we would really like close family and friends only," I say, watching their eyes simultaneously grow wider.

"We were thinking," Brittany hesitates, "if it's okay with you, that maybe you would be willing to let us have the wedding here?"

That is it. The final straw. Mom bursts into tears, racking sobs that cause Grady to stop building and stare while my dad rubs her back gently, shaking his head and mouthing apologies to us.

Brittany looks at me in panic, and I just shrug helplessly. I can't tell if Mom's reaction is good or bad.

Mom takes a few deep breaths to try and calm herself, and she finally chokes out, "I'm just s-s-s-so hap-p-p-y."

I roll my eyes in exasperation and Brittany giggles in relief, getting up and sitting on the couch next to Mom, hugging her. "We are happy too."

Mom clings to her like she is drowning and, eventually, Dad and Grady go back to their Legos.

Finally, Mom wipes her face and says, "There's so much to do! Brittany, I need you to tell me exactly what you want and I'll handle

CHAPTER 22

everything." In sudden swiftness, she gets up and pulls Brittany along with her to the kitchen. I think about going after them, but I chicken out and join the Lego party instead. Much easier.

"Smart move," Dad murmurs as I join them.

"We need to talk about Christmas. No more than three gifts," I say lowly.

Dad grunts. "That's going to be challenging."

"I know. That's why I'm mentioning it to you first," I say obviously, and he nods in understanding.

"You know you aren't paying right?" Dad says casually.

"Brittany would like us to pay for the wedding, and I'm inclined to agree with her," I reply carefully.

"We'll call it a wedding present," he says unconcerned with my hesitation.

"I'll talk to her, but she isn't used to our kind of...generosity," I warn.

"She'll get used to it," he returns matter of fact.

I keep bargaining. "Okay, I'm willing to give you the wedding, but Christmas is a hard limit."

He nods in acquiescence. "Harsh but fair. I can respect that. Eight gifts at Christmas, plus a stocking."

I shake my head. "Three gifts, no stocking."

"Three gifts and a stocking," he counters.

"Two gifts and a stocking or three gifts, no stocking," I counteroffer.

He tries to stare me down. "Four gifts, no stocking."

I don't blink. "Three gifts and a stocking, final offer."

"Done," he nods.

If there's one thing my father can't resist, it's a negotiation.

Two hours later, we leave my parent's house, two boxes of Legos built and my Mom declaring in joy she will handle everything for the wedding. Brittany sighs deeply in relief as we get into the truck. "That went well I think." She relates optimistically, "I wrote down all my requests, and she was very respectful. Then she asked me maybe a million questions and showed me a thousand pictures to get my tastes before declaring she would make it perfect."

I smile fondly. "Sounds like Mom. Thanks for letting her do that by the way. She's literally having the time of her life," I say gratefully.

Brittany smiles with the delight of a child who has gotten out of doing her chores. "I'm getting married and all I have to do is buy a dress and show up? Sign me up!" she laughs.

"By the way, my Dad is insisting on paying, as a wedding gift," I say lightly, emphasizing the word gift.

"That's a generous gift," she mumbles uncomfortably.

"It's kind of how they do things," I say apologetically.

Brittany presses her lips closed and looks out the window. I reach for her hand, intertwining our fingers. "Hey, if you aren't comfortable with it, I'll talk to them."

Brittany heaves a heavy sigh. "I just don't want my parents to feel bad."

"I get that, but we don't have to tell your parents, right? It'll just be a private gift." I squeeze her arm in understanding.

"I guess." Brittany doesn't sound convinced, but she drops it.

Instead of going home, we head to the putt-putt course, and then to a movie at the drive-in theatre two towns over. I place a blow-up mattress in the back of my truck with some pillows and blankets, and we eat junk food and watch a double feature under the stars. Grady falls asleep halfway through the first movie, after declaring it was the best day ever. We stayed through the end of the second movie, snuggling close and enjoying the time together before going home to our separate houses for the night. Thankfully, that nonsense will be coming to an end soon.

Chapter 23

Brittany

"Brittany Masters, what is that I see catching the light?" Lily calls as she walks through the doors of the oncology unit on Thursday. The hospital reorganized the nursing staff again, so we are either assigned to the unit or the clinic, on night shift or day shift. Fingers crossed, this reorg is the one that sticks.

Since Lily stopped coming for treatments, I requested a day shift on the hospital unit instead of in the clinic. That doesn't mean Lily has stopped coming on Thursdays, though. She comes every Thursday to have lunch together. Adding to the tradition, every Thursday she brings the entire unit nursing staff a special treat. One day it was donuts, one day it was pizza, one day it was gift baskets of scented bath soaps and lotions. Today it looks like cupcakes.

I smile at her approach and hold up my hand, doing a little dance.

"I'm so happy for you, Brittany," she says excitedly as she sets the cupcake boxes down on the nurses' station and hugs me.

"Thank you," I say, noting that my arms go around her more easily. I hadn't realized how much weight she's lost recently. Before going to lunch, she greets each nurse, CNA, assistant, and even the occasional wandering doctor by name before insisting they have a cupcake or two.

I watch her work the room. The nurses love her. She asks about their kids and pets before thanking each one for their dedicated service. When she is done, I snag a cupcake and take her arm, threading mine through hers, and lead her to the elevator down to the cafeteria for lunch.

"I'm wondering if you would be my Matron of Honor?" I ask when we settle into our seats.

Lily's eyes lit up and fill with tears. "Of course I will be! How special! Tell me everything. I want to hear every detail," she insists, pushing aside her tray without touching the food, sipping on a bottled water instead.

I detail the proposal for her as accurately as I can, then I quickly run through the wedding details we have so far. It's a shocking amount, really. Grace has texted or emailed me every single day to approve choices, checking things off her list weekly. It's been a total breeze on my end. Something tells me I should buy Cal a day at the spa or whatever the male equivalent is when all this is over, though.

Lily appropriately tears up when I relay the engagement story, and oohs and ahhs over the current wedding plans. I realize that going through everything has prevented me from eating much of my lunch yet, but Lily doesn't have an excuse for her untouched meal.

"Why aren't you eating?" I ask suspiciously.

She wrinkles her nose in distaste. "Food doesn't really taste anymore. I don't have an appetite, and I get sick a lot."

"Have some fruit. Some bananas. It'll settle your stomach," I instruct with concern.

"I'm so glad I'm going to make the wedding." Then she says wistfully, "I can't wait to see you walk down the aisle."

"I'm excited too," I admit. "Everyone is ready. Grady is beside himself. I'm just so glad we will get to spend the holidays as a family."

"Wow, I'm so proud of you, Brittany. Look how far you've come.

CHAPTER 23

You're even stronger now, but with a new...confidence in yourself. You're all a glow. It's wonderful to see," she says emotionally.

"Aw, Lil," I say taking her hand.

"Don't mind me. I'm just getting ultra-sentimental," she says waving her hands in front of her face to prevent tears.

"So what's going on with you?" I ask, trying to lighten the mood.

Lily releases a breath in a puff and rolls her eyes to the ceiling as if things at home are still challenging. "Joe is coping much better now. He still hovers, but he is doing a lot better, I think. Mom thinks the weight loss is absolutely wonderful, although she mentioned that I looked a little too-thin last week."

"Any thoughts on when you'll tell them?" I ask because it'll be getting obvious soon.

"After the holidays and the new year. I think I've got until after then, and I don't want to ruin the holidays," she says softly.

"Then you need to eat more. Not this," I gesture to her sandwich and chips. "Stick to soup, broth, things like that. Nutrients that won't make you sick. Think about drinking a protein shake or a nutritional supplement shake if you don't feel like eating."

She nods. "That's actually a good idea. I'll look into it." Then she smiles and changes the subject. "So tell me, what are my duties as Matron of Honor? Should I host a shower for you?" she plots excitedly.

"I think it's too late for all that. I really don't want a big fuss. Just standing with me at the wedding will work," I insist. Lily eyes me as if she's trying to determine my sincerity. "Seriously," I say sternly, "No showers. No bachelorette party. I'm good."

She nods, but I can't help but notice she corners a few nurses when we get back to the floor, pulling them aside to conspire in whispers before leaving.

Chapter 24

Brittany

The next few weeks are a flurry of wedding planning and preparing both our houses to fit into just mine. When I'm not working, I'm either cleaning out, organizing, and making room in the house for Matt and his things or at Matt's parents' house going over wedding details with his mom, and occasionally my mom. Grady loves these visits because he gets to play with the gigantic amount of toys his new grandparents have bought to ensure his affection for their home. In fact, I'm not entirely sure I would be welcomed if I didn't bring Grady with me. I'm kidding... I'm sure I would. Probably. After a brief interrogation regarding his location.

On a balmy October night, I am exhausted and barely holding my eyes open on the porch swing. We've been so busy we haven't spent much time on the porch lately, and I'm wondering how long it'll take Matt to find me. I left him in the house organizing his closet. As it turns out, it's not that long at all.

"There you are. I couldn't find you in the house," he says, taking a seat next to me and pulling me against his side.

"I'm hiding," I mumble with my eyes drooping closed.

"Not from me I hope," he says, gently pulling his fingers through my

CHAPTER 24

hair.

"From my to do list," I groan.

"Not much left to do but move. You've done a great job." He kisses the top of my head.

I make a sound of contentment.

"It's kind of nice to be back out here. We should take time to do this every night," Matt murmurs.

I would have responded but I'm pretty sure I was already asleep, in my happy place.

* * *

The next day I am stifling a yawn as I walk back to the unit station after doing a round checking on patients only to be pulled into the break room suddenly hearing "surprise" yelled at me by all the shift nurses and Lily.

There are balloons, cake, and gifts, all piled on the breakroom tables. I laugh and hug necks as someone puts a veil on me and a "bride to be" sash. Some of the nurses rotate in and out as I open gifts, and we cut the cake because work doesn't stop for a party.

"I told you no showers," I say mockingly, chiding Lily.

She gives me an innocent "who, me?" look. "Would you really deny me the last chance to ever throw a shower?"

I laugh. "Geez, Lil, you are getting better and better at playing the death card."

She grins shamelessly. "It's the only card I have."

"Thank you, this is great," I say sincerely with a hug.

"It just something pretty simple, but this is how I thought you would want it," she explains simply.

"It's perfect," I say, hugging her again, and then I snap a picture with her so I can have this memory forever.

Chapter 25

Matt

After weeks of preparation, all my stuff has been moved into Brittany's house, and my parents' backyard has been transformed into something my mother calls "Autumn Dreamscape."

I pace the room upstairs in my parents' house and look down at the yard below. Activity buzzes around the party tent. Servers are setting up stations and florists are placing flowers on every stable surface, even creating surfaces to put flowers on where there aren't any. My mom is running around pointing and directing, having the time of her life. I shake my head, imagining Maddy working with Mom on her own wedding. I don't want to be anywhere near that catastrophe waiting to happen. I'm sure the sound barrier would be shattered and decibels only dolphins can hear would result from the shouting and arguing sure to ensue. I say a silent prayer of thanks again that Brittany is so easy going with letting my mom have her fun.

"Matt, sit down. You are going to wear a hole in the floor," Dad says from behind me.

I ignore him and keep pacing.

"Matt, can Grady hang out with you? He got bored with us," Maddy sticks her head in the door to ask, letting Grady into the room.

"Absolutely, Buddy. You look great. Come here," I say, hugging him tight.

"You and Mama are getting married today," he says proudly.

"Yup. You excited?" I ask with an amused smile.

"Yeah!" he says enthusiastically.

"Come on, Grady, let's go find some Legos to distract Matt." Dad takes Grady's hand and leads him downstairs.

I go back to pacing, occasionally looking out the window.

"Sheesh. It's a mad house out there, man," Derek says as he walks in. "Your mom is kind of scary, you know that right?"

I just nod. The thought of Maddy's wedding returns, except now I'm picturing Derek as the groom dealing with Mom. The idea makes me smile since Derek and his dad didn't take it easy on me.

"You nervous?" Derek asks, watching me.

I shake my head. "Big day, that's all."

Derek smirks but nods. I don't know why, but it irritates me. Mr. Calm and Collected never lets anything ruffle his feathers.

"You see Maddy?" I ask just to goad him.

He tenses. "Maybe in passing. Why?"

I eye him in amusement. "No reason."

He looks away and clears his throat but looks suitably shaken at the mention of Maddy. I smile again, anticipating the coming months after Maddy moves home. She hasn't announced anything yet, but she's already asked if she can live in my house. It should be mildly entertaining watching her and Derek avoid each other.

"Cool, Legos!" Derek says with a grin as Grady and Dad come back in the room.

I smirk thinking "why not?" It'll take my mind off things for a few minutes. I sit with the guys as we start putting together a scene from Batman. I have to say, my Dad has good taste in Legos.

An hour later, Maddy laughs as she walks into the room. "Legos?

CHAPTER 25

Really guys? Whatever. Come on, it's show time."

My eyes bug as I stand. Maddy walks over to me and straightens my tie, glancing me over from head to toe.

"You look good. It's going to be fine. Don't lock your knees, and focus on Brittany. You got this. It's a good day; you are becoming a family," she murmurs as she looks into my eyes and pins my boutonniere.

I clear my throat, focusing on her words to calm my heart rate. Becoming a family. A family with Brittany and Grady. Grady's Dad. Brittany's husband. I blow out a breath repeating this in my head. It's a good day. I'm good.

"Aunt Maddy, can I have a flower too?" Grady asks.

"Absolutely, little man. Come here." Maddy kneels and pins him, murmuring to him something I can't concentrate on enough to hear, but Grady looks very serious as he nods along.

"Daddy, your turn," my sister says as she stands and picks up another flower. "I put an extra handkerchief in Mom's clutch, and I'm giving you one too. She's going to need them."

"Thanks, Sugar, you're the best," Dad says before kissing her on the cheek.

"Best for last?" Derek asks as he steps toward her.

She snorts as she avoids eye contact, approaching him without speaking.

"I don't get an inspirational speech?" Derek asks pointedly, teasing her.

Maddy rolls her eyes in irritation and continues to ignore him, pinning his boutonniere with as little contact as possible. Derek stares, trying to catch her gaze with his and failing miserably. He looks quite disgruntled when she takes a step back without sparing him a glance. I smirk. Oh yeah, entertaining indeed.

"Okay!" she claps, turning her back on Derek. "That's everybody. Let's go. Grady, honey, you come with me. Matt, you, Derek, and Daddy down front."

It's a miracle I don't fall down the stairs; my knees are having trouble working. I walk outside and through the back of the tent, then up the aisle followed by my guys, and take my place at the front.

How long do they make you stand up here? Because it genuinely feels like an eternity. When the piano music starts (yes, my mother brought in a baby grand piano), Mom comes in, followed by Brittany's mom.

The music stops, and then starts up again in another piece, and my heart starts pounding. Lily and Maddy come up the aisle and take their place up front before I see her.

Brittany is a vision, floating down the aisle on her dad's arm in a lacey, off-white dress. On her other side, she holds hands with Grady, letting him walk her down the aisle. I notice him concentrating on not stepping on her dress, and I smile. I smile big. There is nothing to be nervous about.

I can't stop staring at Brittany, and she can't look away from me either. We grin goofily at each other, and I'm not even following the service.

We repeat our vows, and when we exchange rings, before the preacher announces us husband and wife, I make vows to Grady about being his daddy. Brittany tears up, and although I know Grady doesn't understand right now, I hope he will eventually. It's important for me to show them both how much I love them.

The preacher announces us man and wife, and we kiss; then he announces us a family: Mommy and Daddy and son. The three of us walk down the aisle, Grady hopping happily between us holding each of our hands. Brittany and I kiss over his head when we get to the end of the aisle just because we can't wait any longer.

Chapter 26

Brittany

"Grady, please. We don't have time. I have to get you to school," I say, losing patience.

Grady's response is to wail incoherently even louder.

He'd been a champ through the whole first semester of first grade, the wedding, and staying three days with Gran and Pop while Matt and I went on our brief but amazing honeymoon. At some point the week before Thanksgiving, he just lost it. He has been grouchy and cranky half the week, and now today's complete melt down before school.

"What's the problem?" Matt asks, rushing to get ready for school too. He is already late as it is.

"I don't know," I mumble, tortured.

Matt sits on the bed and pulls Grady into a hug. "What's the matter, Buddy?"

"I don't wanna go to school!" he cries.

"You love school," Matt replies, rubbing his back.

"Matt, you have to go, you're already late," I say miserably. "Do you not feel well, Grady?"

Grady shakes his head. I feel his forehead and he feels warm. "Lay down, I'll go get the thermometer," I say as I leave the room.

Matt lays Grady down and kisses him, following me out the door. "You got this or do you need me to call in?" he offers.

"I got it. You go. It's easier for me to get off work," I say logically. He nods, although he doesn't look happy about it. To be honest, I'm not super happy about it either. We've only been married a couple of weeks, but the thought of dealing with a weepy and inconsolably sick Grady without Matt makes me weepy and inconsolable. He kisses me, adding "Text me updates."

"Absolutely." I kiss him again.

Matt follows me into Grady's room and kisses him once more. "I love you, Grady. Feel better, okay? Be good for Momma."

I put the thermometer in Grady's mouth and wait the ninety seconds until it beeps. 101.7. Definitely a temperature.

"Does anything hurt?" I ask Grady as he whimpers and shifts around in bed.

He points to his ear. Great. I call the doctor and make an appointment. I call in sick to work and then change out of my scrubs.

"Come on, Buddy, let's go to the doctor," I say when I've changed. Grady starts crying again, and I pray for patience as he reaches frantic-level tears. "You aren't getting shots, Buddy. He's is just going to look in your ears."

That calms him somewhat, but what he says next guts me. "Momma, do you think Daddy is mad at me for crying?" he asks in a choppy voice, hiccupping through more tears.

"No, of course not," I say with surprise, wondering where in the world that came from.

"So you think he still loves me?" he asks with great concern.

I immediately stop and get on my knees so I'm at his eye level. I'm horrified he doesn't already know this, or if he does, that he doubts this in any way. "Grady, both me and Daddy will love you always, no matter what. No matter if you cry, or get sick, or get hurt, or get bad grades, or

CHAPTER 26

make mistakes. We will always love you. Always," I say earnestly.

His relieved nod makes me feel better, but I still want to talk to Matt about this when he gets home.

* * *

It is indeed an ear infection. I text Matt the update, then call in to work to take the next day off too. It is already Thursday, and I am certain Grady won't be over this by Friday. I call Lily and give her the news, and she offers to stop by the house instead of my hospital unit.

"Thanks for coming. Sorry about the change in plans. The girls at work will miss you," I say as I hug her.

"Oh, I already went by. I went down there to take them their treat before I came here," she says with a smile. "I'm sorry Grady isn't feeling well, though," she says with concern.

"He'll be fine. Thanks for bringing lunch. So what was the treat today?" I ask out of curiosity.

Lily's eyes twinkle. "Mani/pedi gift cards." She hands me an envelope and I find it filled with leftover gift cards. I look at her questioningly and she explains, "Use them for yourself, or for nurses who were out today and didn't get one, or nurses on other floors. They're yours."

I smile and hug her in thanks. I don't want to know what kind of budget she has for this whole "weekly treat" thing.

We sit at the kitchen table and I tell her about the wedding, honeymoon, and our bliss the past week and a half since being back, minus Grady's sickness today.

"Are you off on Thanksgiving?" she asks.

I do a tiny happy dance in my chair. "Yep! And the day after too! I can't wait."

"Joe and I are hosting the family again. I'm excited, but Joe is worried about my energy level. I don't really care, though. It's the last one, you know," she says with heartfelt intention.

I nod in understanding but look away. I don't want to think about that. "So what are you making?"

She rattles off a long list, then details her preparation schedule, and I can't help but feel tired just listening to her.

"You should pace yourself, Lil. Don't get over tired," I say with concern.

"I will. My mom is coming to help, and Joe will be there too. I can't wait. I want it to be really special."

I smile and warn again, "Don't put too much pressure on yourself. It'll be special just to have the family together."

She nods guiltily. "I know, I keep reminding myself of that. I can't help it, I just want everything to be perfect."

I understand. I guess the stakes for her are a little higher this year, trying to provide her family with positive memories to last a lifetime.

Grady wakes up from his nap and I bring him in to the kitchen to visit with Lily and eat some chicken noodle soup from Chick-fil-A (and maybe a nugget or two).

Lily rises about an hour later. "Well, I should probably go. I'm so glad I got to visit with you and Grady today," she says sincerely.

I hug her tight and walk her to the door. "Love you, Lil."

* * *

The only thing worse than a grouchy Grady is a sick Grady. And the only thing worse than a sick Grady is a sick Grady that requires any type of eye or ear drops.

He has been in relatively good humor this evening since Matt got home. I am too. Everything is better with Matt here. I make us dinner

CHAPTER 26

and we eat, and then Grady takes his bath. After bath, I can't delay any longer. It is time for medicine.

"He hates drops," I tell Matt worriedly.

"Can't say I blame him," Matt says in commiseration.

That counted as my warning. I call Grady into the kitchen and, as soon as he spots the box, he starts screaming and crying. Matt hugs him close and tries to hold his head still, but it takes both of us twenty minutes to get it done. Meanwhile, I'll have to have my ears checked because Grady's screams reached pterodactyl-level at some point and there might be permanent damage.

I move to hug Grady when we are done, but he snuggles closer to Matt. "I want Daddy!" he wails.

This tears straight through my heart like a knife. I stand frozen, staring at him and Matt, with Matt eyeing me worriedly before he finally picks Grady up and says, "Kiss Momma goodnight. Time for bed."

Grady hides his face from me, but I kiss his head and tell him I love him. Then I head directly to the garage for a fudge pop and sit out on the porch swing, not bothering to stop my tears. About thirty minutes later, the front door opens and Matt steps out, carrying another fudge pop.

"Thanks," I sniffle as he hands it to me.

"You know, he just isn't feeling well. He didn't mean anything by it," Matt says softly.

"I know, but at the same time, it's the first time in seven years that he's sick and doesn't want me. Actually, it's the first time in seven years he doesn't want only me." The tears start anew.

Matt picks me up and puts me on his lap, holding me close to his chest while swaying us back and forth. I notice he is deploying the same technique with me as he does with Grady, soft back rubs while murmuring quiet and comforting love into my ears.

"You know he loves and adores you. That will never change. It's just that now he wants me sometimes too," Matt says gently.

I shudder with emotion. "My head knows that, and I'm so happy for that. Honestly, I am, but my baby is growing up and..." I stop amid a flood of tears.

"It's okay, we will figure this out. It's still a bit new, that's all." Matt continues the rubbing and soothing until my tears stop completely.

"You didn't know you would be holding both of us as we cried tonight, did you?" I ask with a wry grin.

"Fine by me. I wasn't exactly happy to leave you both this morning. Been a rough day for everybody," he admits with a heavy sigh.

I nuzzle into his neck and start kissing him, in that sweet spot that makes him growl.

"Feeling better?" he asks with a grin.

"Mhmm. I have the best husband and father of my child in the world," I say against his neck.

With that, no more words are spoken as he picks me up and carries me into the house to our room.

Chapter 27

Brittany

Having the wedding quickly so we could spend the holidays as a family turns out to be the smartest decision we've ever made. Thanksgiving is wonderful, having brunch with my family and an early dinner with Matt's.

It is at Thanksgiving with Matt's family that Maddy announces she is officially moving home during the Christmas holidays. We also have a very serious talk with his parents about Christmas gifts, which goes over much more easily than I expected, so I suspect Matt has already run interference for us. It still feels a little too easy to me, but Matt assures me everything will be fine.

After the best Thanksgiving yet, we are all looking forward to Christmas.

* * *

Matt

Brittany shares that it was too easy to get my parents to agree to her Christmas gift giving wishes. I didn't tell her before about the negotiation with my Dad, so I don't disagree with her, but I do hold a certain confidence that our wishes will be respected.

Turns out Brittany is right. Looking back, I should have been a little more concerned when we finished Christmas dinner and came into the family room, with only two of the previously agreed upon three gifts under the tree for Grady.

Now, Maddy and Brittany sit together on the sofa, continuing a conversation about her moving schedule and how Maddy will be redecorating my "drab" house. I fight not roll my eyes. Only Maddy would think my house is drab. She is obsessed with bright, bold colors. Mom snaps a picture of them on the couch chatting, and I smile. I love that my sister and my wife get along so well. I can't be happier that Brittany and Grady fit into our family so well.

"Okay, who wants to start opening gifts?" Mom calls.

Grady just about has a conniption fit until Brittany calms him with a few words.

"Matt, help your Dad pass out the gifts," Mom instructs while she puts everyone exactly where she wants them. She is the queen of optimizing camera angles for the holiday photos and videos.

"Dad, why are there only two gifts?" I ask quietly behind the tree.

"Oh there are three. Trust me."

That's when the dread hits. Maybe I should have pulled Brittany aside to warn her right then and there. Maybe that would have helped diffuse the situation before it started. Unfortunately, we'll never know.

We all open our gifts in typical family chaotic fashion. I receive my third "World's Best Teacher" mug and a tool I told Dad I would need for updating our house. I don't know what Brittany and Maddy get,

CHAPTER 27

but they squeal and put their heads together to compare in excitement before throwing their arms around Mom.

Once everyone has settled down and Grady is playing quietly with the superhero city set he'd gotten, Mom hits us with it.

"You know, Grady, I think Santa left something else for you," she calls with a gleam in her eye.

Although I don't meet Brittany's gaze, I can feel her staring me down from across the room.

Grady gets up and goes to Mom, who is pointing excitedly toward the door where my Dad is wheeling in a red Radio Flyer wagon filled to overflowing with toys. I glance at Brittany to see her eyes widen in shock and her face flush. I shake my head in disappointment at my parents, who look less than repentant.

"Really, son, I'm shocked you thought your mother wouldn't find a loophole," Dad tells me with amusement. "Start from the top. If you pull that from the bottom, it'll all fall on you," Dad coaches as he walks over to help Grady.

Great. Grady and Brittany's first Christmas with my parents and he's in danger of a toy avalanche. I can still feel Brittany's eyes on me...and not in a good way. I sheepishly met her eyes and shrug helplessly.

Maddy nudges my wife and murmurs into her ear, damage control under way. I will have to thank her for that later. I escape to the kitchen for no reason other than being afraid that Brittany's stare will literally light me on fire. I'll go in and face the music in a minute; I just need to regroup and think of a way to play it.

"Ow!" I jump at a pinch to my arm. I turn to find Brittany standing before me with her hands on her hips. She doesn't say anything; she just stares up at me disapprovingly.

"Look," I sigh, "We talked to them both and they agreed. I didn't know she found a loophole."

Thankfully, Brittany grins despite her stern demeanor. "A loophole?"

"My dad and I agreed to three gifts and a stocking." I lift my arms helplessly. "She found a loophole."

Brittany drops her arms and smiles cheerfully with a hint of mischievous trouble. "I'm not upset with you. In fact, I'm not upset at all."

I eye her with all the skepticism I feel at her statement.

"Really, I'm not. I'm annoyed that they went out and did the thing we asked them not to do. I'm a little hesitant to ever leave him alone with them for fear of death by spoiling, but I'm not upset." She puts her arms around me to prove it, and like a dope so ready to believe the unbelievable, I hold her tight and kiss her like she deserves.

She lays her head on my chest. "Merry Christmas, Matt."

"Merry Christmas, baby. Thank you for not being upset."

She beams up at me and pulls out of my arms. "Of course. Although, I can't say your mother won't be upset when you tell her all that is staying here at her house."

My mouth drops open as she pats my chest and crosses the kitchen back toward the living room.

I groan. Merry freaking Christmas to me.

**

"Absolutely not!" Mom screeches.

"We can't even get all that in the car, Mom. We aren't taking it with us," I say firmly.

"That's why I told you to bring the truck," she grumbles as Dad enters the kitchen.

"What's going on?" he asks.

"They are refusing to take Grady's gifts with them," Mom tattles. Much to her annoyance, Dad's eyes glitter with respect.

CHAPTER 27

"We told you guys not to go overboard. You did. He's not taking all that home with us. Even if we could get it all in the car, where are we supposed to put it?" I argue.

Mom and Dad exchange a look I don't even want to try and decipher as Brittany comes into the kitchen.

"We are so thankful for your generosity, but it's too much for Grady. He needs to learn to appreciate what he has, and we are afraid he won't if he is given mountains of toys," she says eloquently in a calming tone that instantly settles Mom.

"That's why we respectfully asked you to keep it to three gifts and a stocking," I can't help but point out.

Mom puts a finger in my face. "You and your father agreed to that. I did not."

"Mom..." I groan in frustration.

"The toys will stay here, in the fort out back," Dad announces with finality.

All eyes swivel to him.

"The fort?" I question.

"Out back?" Brittany asks suspiciously.

"I thought the fort fell down?" I ask in confusion.

Mom looks at Dad, a little guiltily. Oh no.

"We are building a new one for Grady," she says simply, with a tipped chin daring me to argue.

"Say what now?" Brittany asks me in disbelief.

"There was an old outbuilding on the property when we bought it, out in the edge of the woods. Matt and Maddy used to play in it, but it fell down a few years ago. We are just going to build something simple for Grady, *and other grandchildren*, to play in," Dad explains with a suggestive wink.

"You're building Grady a house?" Brittany blinks in astonishment.

Mom and Dad grin and trade that look again, the one that makes me hope and pray this is the last surprise for today. "Actually, we are building him a playhouse," Dad clarifies.

"Although it will have water and electricity. But it's not like we are gifting it to him; it'll be for the others too," Mom further adds.

Brittany nods woodenly. "Well, thank you for not giving my son a house. Matt?" she tugs me out of the kitchen to the hall powder room and pushes me inside. "Why do I think that your parents say playhouse but mean guest house?" she whispers, crowding me against the counter.

"Because you're catching on?" I say with a faint smile.

Brittany opens and closes her mouth several times before sighing. "We have got to get them under control. Seriously, Matt. Can you imagine when we have more kids?"

I smile. We have discussed having more kids briefly, but I like that it's now a foregone conclusion. "It'll be fine. We just need to strategize."

"Strategize?" she asks in confusion.

"Maybe we always make them come to us. That way they can only bring what they can fit in the car."

Brittany stares at me for a moment before laughing hysterically. I take advantage of her good humor to make out with her before rejoining the rest of the family. After a few minutes, when I think Brittany may finally have gotten the idea of how much I love her, I smile and tug her out of the powder room. "Come on, we can't leave Grady with Maddy for too long or she'll teach him highly inappropriate things."

Brittany follows, giving Dad the eye until he looks a little sheepish about allowing Mom's "loophole." We stay at my parents' until Grady passes out from all the excitement, surrounded by a mountain of gifts.

Chapter 28

Brittany

The Christmas holiday break is a total blur. Between school programs for both Matt and Grady, a work party, family reunions, and moving Maddy into Matt's house next door, we are completely exhausted by the time the new year rolls around. Thankfully, I have some time saved up and Matt and Grady are out of school until the second week in January, so I take the first week of the month off to spend with them.

We help Maddy get settled into Matt's house, take a couple of day trips, and are just lazy around the house. We play games and watch movies, eating pizza on the floor in the living room. It is bliss.

However, there is a harsh reality waiting for me when I go back to work the second week in January. I walk onto the floor and head straight for the break room to stow my stuff. Upon entering the room, I find a table full of doughnuts and carafes of coffee. I grin and wonder if Lily has upped her treat days for the holidays or if another patient is the benefactor.

I walk to the nurse's station to log in and go over shift change with the nurse manager ready to go off duty. I am greeted by several nurses with sad smiles.

"Why does everyone look so sad?" I ask Trina, the nurse manager

I'm working with.

She stares at me. "You don't know?"

A sinking feeling starts in my gut. "Lily?"

She nods sadly, telling me, "She was brought in last night."

We go through shift change procedures and then she personally walks me through Lily's chart. As our teams change shifts, we work to get everyone squared away. Most of my team instantly recognizes Lily's name on the board.

"We can handle this for a while if you want to go in there," Hannah, one of my nurses, says with a hand on my shoulder.

"I have a few things to do, then I'll go. Y'all don't crowd the family," I say in a voice that is more authoritative than I feel.

Hannah nods sadly and walks away. I keep busy in my office until I can force myself to look over Lily's chart again. There are several physical reasons for her admittance, lots of medical jargon. Her liver is shutting down, her gastroenterology system is producing too much acid due to tumors in her intestines. The long and short of it is, the end is near.

"Gonna hide in here all day?" Pam, another of my nurses, asks, leaning her hip against the door. Pam is one of the older nurses and has taken a little bit of a maternal role on the team.

"Maybe," I say stubbornly, putting my head in my hands.

"Suck it up. The family needs to see you," she says roughly.

My head snaps up. "Is she okay?"

"No. Her family just found out, and suddenly it's the end. They don't need us. They need you. So get in there."

She's right.

I check in at the station before walking over to Lily's room. I knock lightly before opening the door. Joe is there with Lily's mom and dad, and three of my nurses who are currently supposed to be doing rounds.

My staff catch my eye and scoot out before I can let the door close. Lily

CHAPTER 28

is smiling at me. "I was wondering when you would have a minute."

I smile affectionately as I approach her bed. "You're spoiling my staff. They aren't worth anything with you in here."

Lily chuckles unrepentantly. "It's the least we can do. Right, Joe?"

Joe nods in agreement enthusiastically. "Absolutely. Anything you guys need."

"Hi, Brittany." Lily's mom comes to give me a stiff hug.

"Hey there. Sorry to see you guys under the circumstances," I say softly.

She nods sadly, and I wave to Lily's dad sitting in the corner.

"Brittany, come sit with me and tell me about your first holidays together as a family," Lily commands and pats her bed.

I perch on the side politely. "You will not believe the mountain of presents the Knight's got Grady."

Lily giggles. "You said their agreement came too easy. I hope you got pictures."

I smile at the memory. "I did, and I do."

I spend the next forty-five minutes detailing our Christmas festivities to Lily with flourish, just to see her smile and laugh. I continue until there is a light knock on the door and Hannah sticks her head around the curtain. "Brittany?"

I turn to her professionally and get up. "I'll come back after lunch, Lil. I want to hear about your holidays." She smiles in acknowledgement as I wave to her parents and get back to work.

A few hours later, when I make it back to Lily's room, she is reading in bed while Joe dozes lightly on the couch. I notice the nurses rarely leave Lily alone in her room, each of them taking turns sitting with her and regaling her with stories.

"Hey," I whisper, trying not to wake Joe.

Lily smiles and puts her book down, patting the side of her bed again.

I lay down beside her and intertwine our arms.

"How are you?" I ask softly so I don't wake Joe.

Lily sighs tiredly. "I'm okay."

"In pain?"

"Not really. You guys are giving me the good stuff. Uncomfortable, maybe." I can tell there's more she wants to say but she doesn't.

"And your family?"

She frowns. "They're pretty upset. I barely made it through Christmas. In fact, I told the family last week. Mom wouldn't speak to me until Joe brought me in last night."

I grip her hand as tears fall down her cheeks. "It's gonna be okay, Lil. They are just processing. You remember how it was with Joe. They'll come around."

She nods but says, "This is so hard for them."

"It's hard for you too," I say pointedly.

She looks at me through watery eyes. "I've had the most time to adjust, but it's still hard. Especially knowing how much pain this is causing everyone else."

I hug her tight and whisper, "Just keep focusing on giving everyone positive memories before you go. You did so good, Lil. You gave everyone almost a whole year of great memories."

She takes a deep breath and nods in agreement. "You're right, that's a good thing to focus on."

We lay in silence for a while, holding each other close. Finally, when Joe starts to stir, I pull back and give her a final hug.

"I should get back to work. Call me if you need me," I whisper, giving her hand a final squeeze.

She nods before I turn to leave. I'm feeling a little lost with the tables turned. I am so used to Lily being the fountain of strength and wisdom. I'm just not sure if I can handle it being me.

Then it strikes me. It's going to have to be me. Lily is dying.

CHAPTER 28

* * *

When I get home that night, I only want to collapse on the couch. It's been a long and emotional day.

"Hey, baby, how was your day?" Matt greets me as I walk in late to the kitchen. He is gorgeous and cooking dinner while my son plays in the living room. My heart could burst, especially after a day like today. I smile faintly, weekly offering, "Getting better."

"You okay?" he asks with concern, seeing my dejected self.

"Lily's in my unit. She's not doing well. It was a long and emotional day."

Matt drops the spoon he is holding to give me a long hug. I hold on tight for as long as I can. Maybe I won't have to be a fountain of strength. Maybe Matt can be my fountain of strength.

"Dinner's ready. Wanna set the table?" he asks giving me a final squeeze.

"Grady, want to come set the table?" I call with a wink to Matt as I sink into a chair at the bar, watching Matt finish cooking.

"Is Aunt Maddy coming for dinner?" he asks as Matt hands the plates down.

I chuckle. Maddy has been crashing our dinners pretty much since she moved in next door. We don't mind; we love it. "Better set a place just in case."

"Can't believe I remodeled an entire kitchen and she eats all her meals here," Matt grumbles.

"But we love having Maddy over," I counter. "And hey, now that you have the experience, feel free to remodel our kitchen."

He grunts and gripes, but I can tell he is already making plans for his summer break.

Just then, the door opens and we hear, "It's me!"

Matt rolls his eyes while I giggle and call, "Hey, Maddy!"

"Got here just in time for dinner, I see," Matt says as the put-upon older brother.

Maddy laughs. "I have always had a stellar sense of timing," she says unapologetically, sitting in what has now been dubbed "Aunt Maddy's seat" at the table.

"We need to get a bigger table," I muse as I look around at the full-to-bursting oak table, which contains the most precious people in my life. It comfortably seats two, but barely fits the four that our family has grown into.

"Maybe this summer," Matt says with a wink.

"Oooh, if you are gonna remodel, I could help design," Maddy offers excitedly.

"Maddy..." my husband says in warning.

"What? I'm just saying, a little color never hurt anything...."

And they are off, arguing over the finer points of the remodel that Matt did on his house. I listen with a smile, thinking no one has ever been more blessed than me.

"Modern doesn't have to mean colorless. Everyone loves a statement wall," Maddy emphasizes.

"No Maddy, *you* love a statement wall."

"What's it say?" Grady asks around a bite of dinner.

We all look at him questioningly. "What, Buddy?" I ask.

"The statement wall. What's it say?" he clarifies.

We all throw our heads back and laugh. "Exactly, Buddy. It can say whatever you want it to. Unless you don't have a statement wall, then it just says boring," Maddy says, looking directly at her brother.

We finish dinner while Matt and Maddy argue the finer points of interior decorating. Afterwards, Maddy plays with Grady in his room while I write in my Lily journal, still disconcerted with the realization that Lily will soon pass away.

Thumbing through my journal, I go back to the first page. Intention-

CHAPTER 28

ality. Lily was choosing to live her last days intentionally, and she did. The next page, don't fight, let things happen. I reread my entire journal tonight, going back over every single page until I decide I'm not losing my fountain of strength; she is leaving the best parts of herself behind.

Chapter 29

Brittany

Lily's doctor and I, along with my staff and the other shifts of nurses, may have fudged Lily's chart enough to keep her in our unit for her last days instead of moving her to hospice. This turns out to be a little over two weeks. I spend as much time with Lily as I can, visiting in between the other nurses and her family.

I am happy to see her parents seem to have forgiven her for keeping her prognosis to herself. They eventually warm to me and Joe after apparently considering us the enemy for knowing about Lily's condition the whole time. Lily and Joe step up their gifts, making sure each shift of nurses receives some kind of treat or gift every single day that she is in the hospital. I keep trying to talk her out of her extreme gift giving, but all she ever does is smile and say it is the least she could do.

I am working a double shift through the night one night, spending the evening in Lily's room when I'm not needed on the floor, when Lily and I have our final talk. Joe isn't spending the night at the hospital anymore. Lily insisted that since her family spends the days with her, they need to rest at night. With this in mind, I curl up under a blanket on her couch and we talk like we have so many times before, usually on our Thursdays. Lily is pale, lying weakly in her bed as we talk softly.

CHAPTER 29

"I'm sad it took this to put us back in touch," I muse.

"Yeah, I've thought of that too. I will forever be grateful, though. This has turned out to be my favorite byproduct of the cancer," she says with a sweet smile.

"If you wanted to hang out, you could have just asked, you didn't have to go and die." I say dryly.

Lily laughs ironically. "I'll remember that for next time. I'm pleased you've jumped aboard the death card."

I smile; Lily so did love to play the death card. "You're my best friend, Lil," I say sentimentally.

"You're mine, too," she says with a smile. "Thanks for that. Thanks for making time for me when you didn't have to."

"Please," I grunt. "How else were you going to tell me how to live my life? You're my fountain of strength, Lil."

To my surprise, Lily laughs at that. "You're the strongest person I know, Brittany. You are your own fountain of strength. I just gave you a little nudge toward what you already knew was right."

"You know, I have an entire journal of Lily entries that says differently."

"Lily entries?" she asks curiously.

"I wrote down all our visits and the little things you told me."

Lily is quiet for a moment while she stares at me. Finally, she speaks softly, "I have one final thing to tell you, Brittany."

I listen with rapture waiting for her words. What will she say, knowing this is probably going to be the last time we get any length of time together? What would I say in her place?

"Laugh. Make the memories. Live for the moments together." She takes a deep breath and continues on seriously, "And I don't care what anyone says, leggings are not pants."

She lets me sit in stunned silence for about a second before she cracks a grin. I start laughing too, loudly, and she joins in.

Lily. Of course, her last words would be to cut the tension and make me laugh.

* * *

The next morning when driving home, I don't need the radio to stay awake. I'm occupied thinking about my late-night chat with Lily. My mind roams over my memories with her from the past months. When I pull into the driveway, Maddy waves at me as she pulls out of her driveway off to work. The house is lit, and I can hear the activity on the other side of the door as I get out of the car in the garage.

"Hey, guys," I call in greeting.

"Momma!!" Grady shouts, running to me and throwing his arms around me.

Never. Gets. Old.

This time, I fall on my knees and throw my arms around him, hugging him tight and showering his face with kisses.

"Gross, Mom! Too tight!" he whines and squirms away.

I grin and let him go, standing and throwing my arms around my husband. "Good morning," he says, holding me tight. "I missed you last night."

"I missed you too," I say into his chest, holding him even tighter.

"You okay?" he asks, reading my mood.

I reluctantly let him go. "Just really happy to be home."

He smiles tentatively like he doesn't believe me and turns back to the kitchen. "Oatmeal or cereal?" he asks.

"Cereal."

My man pours my cereal and places the bowl in front of me before pouring his own and joining me and Grady at the table.

"You know why breakfast is my favorite meal of the day?" Matt asks.

"Why?"

CHAPTER 29

"Because Aunt Maddy's not here," Grady pipes up around a mouthful of Cheerios.

I laugh and Matt grins. "He gets me, that boy."

Grady finishes his cereal and gets up to take it to the sink. "I won't rat you out," I say with a wink to Matt.

He quirks a brow in question.

"I won't tell anyone how much you adore your little sister, despite your constant teasing," I say standing, kissing his cheek on my way to the sink.

"Ahh, she knows. It's why she's so annoying," he says with mock regret.

I laugh again, heeding Lily's last advice. "I love you," I say dreamily.

He smiles warmly and answers, "I love you too."

Walking over to the sink, Matt puts his arms around me from behind. "We'll continue this conversation tonight?"

"Date night? Are you going to share your plans with me?"

"Nope, I want to surprise you. I'll drop Grady at Gram and Pop's and then come and pick you up."

I smile happily. "Sounds good."

Matt kisses me one final time before calling, "Ready, Grady? Let's go!"

"Coming, Daddy!" he says, flying out the door.

"Hey!" I yell after Grady.

He comes back in, penitent. "Sorry, Mom." He kisses me, then jogs after Matt again.

"Have a good day, I love you!" I yell after him.

A brief wave is all I get before he jumps in the car to be taken to school. I smile as I shut the door and head to bed. Mornings like this are the memories I want to remember the most. Lily is right. Laugh. Make the memories.

And for goodness sakes. Leggings aren't pants.

Epilogue

Brittany

It is a rainy Tuesday in January when Matt and I dress in black to attend Lily's funeral. Grady goes to school as normal, but Matt and I both take a personal day from work so we can be here. In fact, Lily's Mom has asked me to speak. I hesitated at first, and although I felt really uncomfortable I, agreed.

Matt takes my hand as we enter the church and asks, "You okay?"

I nod serenely, taking in the flowers that fill the vestibule and the large portrait of Joe and Lily at the doors to the sanctuary. Photo books of pictures from the past year line the tables. They are Lily's gift to each family member given on the day she told them about the cancer. She'd made them each an album of her favorite memories from recent years, focusing on the last year specifically.

We find a seat, forgoing the usual meeting of the family so I can gather my thoughts before my speech. Speech? Eulogy? Kind words spoken about a loved one?

I clutch my Lily journal in my hand and toy with the pages. I flip through the early ones, remembering how she changed my perspective and helped me open my life. The organ plays and I tear up as Joe leads the processional of close family members into the sanctuary. The service begins with a hymn, followed by the pastor of her church offering opening remarks and a Bible verse.

EPILOGUE

"It is my understanding that Lily became quite close with a family member for the year before she passed. Brittany Knight, a cousin of Lily's, will now come forward to bring a few words about her time with Lily."

Matt rises and offers me a hand up. I slowly stand and walk to the front of the sanctuary, climbing the steps to the platform. It is overwhelming. The church is mostly full, and Joe and Lily's parents are crying in the front row. My own eyes tear as I see my entire nursing staff, and the staff from a few other shifts, sitting in the back-middle section. They must have called in auxiliary staff to cover our shift.

"Lily and I grew up going to the same school, but quickly lost touch," I start with a shaky voice from the podium. I place my hands on top of my Lily journal in an effort to center myself and remember what's important. "I just happened to be working in the clinic when Lily came in for her first treatment. I was shocked and appalled when I saw her chart with her diagnosis. Her treatment plan didn't make sense." I avoid looking at Joe and Lily's parents at all costs, focusing instead on my nursing friends and Matt.

"When I asked her about it, she said she didn't want to spend the last year of her life sick and dying; she wanted to fill it with memories." I smile and gaze at Matt to center me and help me remember the greatest gift she gave me. "I didn't understand. I was upset and tried to change her mind. I felt like she was giving up." I take a deep breath. "But I spoke to my then-neighbor about it, and he said he thought she was brave." I pause.

"Naturally, I was confused, because giving up isn't usually considered brave. He explained that living life on your own terms and having the strength to stare death in the face for the sake of spending unaffected time with your family is brave. That bravery is not always something you do, but sometimes something you don't do."

A tear falls down my cheek and I take another deep breath. I hold up my journal. "I sat with Lily for all her treatments, and when she stopped taking them, we visited every week at least once. I started writing down my memories of our time and the things she was teaching me."

I flip the pages and sigh. "We were the same age, but Lily...Lily was wiser than anyone I've ever met. Lily called me out on my crap. She saw me. She saw my fears and helped me learn how to open myself up. It was my honor to ask her to be my Matron of Honor at my wedding this past November, and I will forever be thankful to Lily for the gifts she gave me. She gave me the gift of healing when I didn't know I needed it. She gave me the gift of confidence in the face of my fears when I didn't know I was afraid, and the gift she gave all of us are the precious memories that we will cherish for the rest of our lives."

There are several sniffles, but I am not done. "I was mad at Lily for not fighting, but that was one of the first pieces of advice she gave me. 'Stop fighting. Let things happen to you. Be open,' she said. Looking now to the back of the room, at half the clinical staff of the Cancer Center here today," I smile, "I think she was right. She touched so many lives intentionally because she knew her time was ending. Our staff adored Lily, and she will be missed, particularly on Thursdays. We carry with us the beautiful memories she gave us as well as the gift of the last year of her life. We hold her lesson to intentionally touch as many people as possible with the time you have left."

With that, I pick up my journal, drop my eyes, and walk back to my seat beside Matt, who puts his arm around me and kisses my temple.

The service continues, but I am lost in thought. When we stand for the processional, I dab my eyes and take deep breaths, trying to gather myself before the graveside service. I'm shocked when Joe stops at Matt and Matt edges out into the aisle, giving Joe direct access to me.

"Thank you, Brittany. Your words were perfect," he says sincerely, giving me a hug.

Speechless, I hug him back. I am shocked again as Lily's mom reached

EPILOGUE

for my hands. I offer them to her, and she tugs me along beside her, clinging to me as we follow the casket and Joe out of the sanctuary.

"Thank you, Brittany, for giving me the perspective I needed," she whispers brokenly as we watch the casket being loaded into the hearse. I squeeze her before she lets go, heading out with her husband, Lily's father. I am thankful that her arms are immediately replaced by Matt's, who guides me to our car.

By the end of the day, after the graveside service and the family meal at the church, Matt and I arrive home in tired silence. It has been a long, emotional day. After Grady gets off the bus, we do homework, eat dinner, and put Grady to bed. Matt and I quietly go out to the front porch swing afterwards.

We sway in silence, me snuggled into his side in the way that marks my happy place.

"I'm thinking about adding some flowers to the yard," Matt says suddenly.

"Oh, yeah?" I ask distractedly.

"Maybe some lilies. Here, by the porch," he points.

I follow his direction, then look up into the eyes of the biggest blessing God ever gave me.

"I think lilies would be perfect," I say before kissing him deeply.

God is the giver of blessings, and I am eternally grateful. Lily taught me how to accept the blessings, and there are no words to describe how indebted I am to her for that.

***

Thank you for reading Summertime Lilies! I hope you enjoyed Brittany and Matt's story. Want to keep reading? Hearts collide when Maddy and Derek meet, but they might just kill each other before they even consider the possibility of giving in to love. Read Book Two in the Oak Street Series, Shut the Front Door here.

About the Author

LM Karen writes contemporary Christian fiction romance. As a long-time lover of words, she can generally be found behind her laptop or with a book in her hand.

Thank you for reading Summertime Lilies, I hope you enjoyed it. If you did, please consider leaving a short review on Amazon.

Keep an eye on my website for new releases: lm-karen-author.mailchimp-sites.com

Follow me on Instagram: @lmkarenauthor

Follow me on Facebook: facebook.com/lmkarenauthor

Sneak Peek!

Book 2 of the Oak Street Series - Maddy and Derek's story can be found here: Shut the Front Door

Enjoy a short sneak peek below:

Shut the Front Door

Derek

I'm starting to officially get angry. Stubborn woman won't return my calls, texts, or emails. Who even emails socially anymore? Desperate people, that's who. Won't see me when I stop by her work and won't answer the door when I go to her house. I can't figure out how she knows when I'm coming, because her door is always locked when I get there; but Grady and Brittany say it's always unlocked when they try it. She's become some kind of ninja at avoiding me.

Seems like she's doubled down on this whole, not dating me thing. I would think at this point I'm coming across as pathetic, but it seems to tick her off. Madison angry is passionate, and passion is good so I'll take it how I can get it. I admit that maybe this is a roundabout way of getting there, but we'll end up where I need us to be sooner or later.

It's been two weeks since that night, and all I can think about is how smart and witty she is, how her lips feel on mine, and how attractive she is when she is yelling at me. I cut my bike off and walk it the rest of the way to Brittany's, parking it on the side of the house where I know Maddy won't see it. I trudge through the door, calling out a greeting and walk in on the family eating some kind of casserole at the kitchen table.

"Want dinner?" Brittany asks motioning to the empty chair known as 'Aunt Maddy's seat.'

"Where's Maddy?" I ask directly, ignoring her offer. It's Friday night, and I'm done messing around. We are settling this *now*. I have never worked so hard on one woman, and if I weren't absolutely certain she was worth it, I would have given up long ago. My game plan has been chucked and I'm winging it from here on out.

Brittany looks at Matt with panicked eyes as Matt shrugs casually, "She's on a date."

I freeze, sure I heard him wrong. "She's what?" I grind out, willing my head not to explode.

"On a date. With some lawyer." Matt says, easily avoiding Brittany's elbow. "Come on," he tells her playfully, "Remember when I wanted to go to a movie and you wanted to stay here? You were right, this is more fun." He says gesturing at me with a grin.

"Matt, we promised." Brittany chides.

"What exactly did you promise?" I ask tightly.

Brittany eyes me and doesn't respond, so I switch my focus to Matt. "She doesn't want us to talk to you about her anymore." He takes another bite of chicken, "But I've never respected my sister's privacy, so whatever."

"Where is she?" I ask again.

Matt looks at Brittany questioningly while Brittany studies her plate without saying a word. My blood pressure is rising by the second.

"I know." Grady offers smugly, "And I didn't make any promises."

I breathe in relief and cross the table to kiss his head, "You are my favorite person in the entire world Grady. Where is she?"

"I want you to take me to a baseball game. A big one." He demands with calculation.

I glance at Matt and Brittany in shock, who look extremely amused and not at all like they are going to help me. "Ok you little extortionist. I'll take you to a game."

"On your bike." Grady says. I know Brittany won't agree to that, so I think fast.

"One minor league game and a trip to the toy store where you get three things, whatever you want, we go in the car." The ridiculousness of the situation is lowering my blood pressure.

"Five things." Grady counters

"Deal." I accept immediately. Don't tell Grady but if he had asked for ten things I would have agreed. Thank God he doesn't realize just how much I need this information, as the art of the deal is based on supply and demand. Hello capitalism and welcome to America.

"Dinner at Luigi's, and they were planning to go to a movie after." Grady announces proudly.

"What movie?"

"I don't know, but at the big theatre with all the colors."

"Thanks buddy" I kiss his head again and glare at my sister and her husband, who look more proud and amused than they have a right to. "You two should be ashamed for raising a blackmailer."

"Negotiator" Matt calls to my back.

I leave without another word, cranking my bike loudly and riding straight to Luigi's.

Thankfully, they are still at the restaurant when I get there. I spot Maddy immediately, looking absolutely gorgeous in a cobalt blue dress that matches her eyes. I don't know who she's with, but he's slightly

SNEAK PEEK!

balding from the back and is in absolutely no way worthy of that dress. My blood pressure is rising again, as another wave of anger hits me. I can't believe she'd rather be out with this guy than me. I stalk up to her table and watch her eyes widen when she notices me.

"Did I not make myself clear?" I ask calmly. Relatively calmly. I mean, as calmly as attainable in my current state.

Her mouth drops open and her eyes dart around nervously, "Are you really making a scene right now?"

I nudge the lawyer over without a word and sit down demanding, "Well?"

Maddy sniffs and tosses her hair, "I don't know what you're talking about." Then she levels her gaze at me, "But I'm fairly certain I made *myself* clear." She says in annoyance.

"Um...do you need a minute?" the guy beside me asks.

"Actually, I can take it from here, thanks for playing." I say tightly without removing my eyes from Maddy.

Her mouth drops open indignantly, "I am on a date. Who do you think you are? You can't speak to him like that."

"I just did. Besides, the only person you are supposed to be on a date with, is *me*." I say with just as much attitude. I'm getting real tired of her stubborn streak. Canyon probably. We've passed streak, it's more like a stubborn canyon.

"I told you I'm not dating you." Maddy says through clenched teeth. Her words protest, but the challenge issued in her eyes is very clear. That's the thing about Maddy. Her words say one thing, but her body says another. I get the feeling she's not exactly lying; she wants to believe herself, but when it comes down to it she doesn't. That's exactly why she needs a little push.

"And I told you, that's not an option. Now tell this man you have an emergency and let's go." I order more angrily than I intend. She has a knack for chipping away at my self-control.

"That's ok, I think I'll just..." he stammers, inching away from me.

"Donald, stay." Maddy says starting to apologize, but I snort, interrupting her.

"Donald?" I say derisively.

Maddy straightens her back, "Now you are just being mean." She shifts to talk to Donald again, "I'm so sorry about this. It seems I may need to handle this though, so maybe we can get together another time?"

Donald nods wordlessly and lets himself out of the other side of the booth.

"Don't count on it, Donald." I taunt as he leaves.

Maddy is glaring at me, "I hope you are happy. You were mean to a perfectly nice man. What, have you resorted to intimidation tactics now?"

She's kidding, right? "You don't return my calls, texts, or emails, won't see me. Then I go over to Brittany's and have to hear from *Grady* that you are on a date? Too far, Madison." I say gravely.

"Snitch" she grumbles, although she has the decency to look embarrassed.

"Have you eaten?" I demand.

"What does it look like? No, we were *very rudely* interrupted before we got our meal." she snaps indignantly.

"Good," I stand and put some bills on the table, holding out my hand, "Come on."

"I'm not going anywhere with you." she insists vehemently.

Nope. I'm done. No more asking nicely. I lean over the booth and put my face close to hers talking low and slow, "You are either walking out, or I'm carrying you out, but we are leaving here together."

Her eyes widen and I can tell by her dilated pupils that it's from excitement and not from fear. She takes my hand silently. I pull her out of the booth and out of the restaurant.

SNEAK PEEK!

* * *

Hearts collide when Maddy and Derek meet, but they might just kill each other before they even consider the possibility of giving in to love. Find the rest of Derek and Maddy's story, Shut the Front Door here.

Made in the USA
Monee, IL
17 July 2025